THE CIDER HOUSE RULES

JOHN IRVING

BASED ON HIS NOVEL *THE CIDER HOUSE RULES*

THE CIDER HOUSE RULES

A SCREENPLAY

NEW YORK

Library of Congress Cataloging-in-Publication Data
Irving, John
The cider house rules : a screenplay / John Irving.
p. cm.
"Based on his novel The cider house rules."
ISBN 0-7868-8523-8
I. Cider house rules (Motion picture) II. Title.
PN1997.C494 1999
791.43'72—dc21 99-39796
CIP

FIRST EDITION

3 5 7 9 10 8 6 4 2

CONTENTS

INTRODUCTION

I began observing surgical procedures of an obstetrical and gynecological kind in 1980; these observations, together with some reading in the medical-history library at Yale, comprised my earliest research for my sixth novel, *The Cider House Rules*, which was published in 1985. In that same year I began work on this screenplay, which I continued for thirteen (now fourteen) years.

Four different directors were attached to the project; none of them was a writer. While the writing is all mine, suffice it to say that the suggestions of these directors have influenced this screenplay, at times in conflicting ways.

The first director, Phillip Borsos, who is dead now, advised me to move the screenplay the farthest distance from the novel; in that version, there was no triangular love story involving Homer, Candy, and Wally, and Homer's only love interest, which was unrequited, was in Mr. Rose's daughter. (In retrospect, these were bad ideas.)

Of the three directors to follow Phillip Borsos, Michael Winterbottom moved the screenplay back closer to the novel, but under Winterbottom's influence the Homer-Candy love affair became too dominant. The final version of the screenplay, which I developed with Lasse Hallström—the fourth director—also reinstated Homer's relationship with Candy, although that relationship is less of a love story than it is in the novel. Homer's relationship with Dr. Larch is the dominant relationship in the Lasse Hallström film, as it should be. (I have addressed these differences, and the process of adapting a screenplay from a novel, in more detail in my memoir *My Movie Business*.)

Naturally, there are a few scenes in the shooting script that were not shot, and many more were cut out of the picture in Lasse's editing process. But the screenplay, as published here, is the version that Lasse and I agreed to shoot upon the commencement of principal photography in September 1998.

For those readers who are familiar with the finished film, you will note that much of the dialogue was slightly adjusted (or improvised) from the dialogue recorded here; also, some of the scenes that remain in the finished film do not appear in the exact same sequence as they are written. I saw no reason to indicate these discrepancies on the page. (It is difficult enough to read a screenplay without such interjections.) A shooting script is not supposed to be a faithful record of what was shot, nor does this script reflect how the film was edited.

Lasse Hallström is Swedish. Given his accent, which I am especially fond of, *great* is an original-sounding word. This is the version of the screenplay to which Lasse said "Great!" This was the point of departure, from where he began to direct the film.

I am the screenwriter; the screenplay is mine. Lasse is the director. The film is his. I've said this before: When I feel like being a director, I write a novel.

—John Irving
June 1999

THE CIDER HOUSE RULES

FADE IN. BEGIN TITLE SEQUENCE.

EXT. ST. CLOUD'S—TRAIN STATION—DAWN

An establishing shot of the rundown train station on an overcast morning. There's snow on the station platform. A train arrives and departs.

LARCH (*V.O.*)

In other parts of the world, young men of promise leave home to make their fortunes, battle evil, or solve the problems of the world.

Behind the station, at the top of the hill, lies the St. Cloud's orphanage.

LARCH (*V.O.*)

I was myself such a young man, when I came to save the orphanage in St. Cloud's . . . many years ago.

EXT. ST. CLOUD'S—ORPHANAGE—EARLY MORNING

A man and woman (COUPLE #1) *make their way toward the main entrance of the large brick building.*

LARCH (*V.O.*)

Here in St. Cloud's, I have come to understand that promises are rarely kept, that the battle isn't so much against evil as ignorance, and that being successful can't hold a candle to being *of use*.

The couple enters the orphanage, where we hear the sound of babies.

LARCH (*V.O.*)

Nor have I solved the problem I came here to solve.

INT. ORPHANAGE—MORNING

Two nurses, EDNA *and* ANGELA, *chase* CHILDREN—*a morning routine.*

LARCH (*V.O.*)

Even in the most enlightened times, unwanted babies will manage to be born. That there will always be orphans is simply not a problem to be solved. Here in St. Cloud's, we don't regard the sordid facts of life as problems.

The camera goes up the stairs with some of the kids.

INT. LARCH'S OFFICE—DAY

We enter an office where DR. LARCH shows couple #1 their newly adopted son, HOMER, *an infant who lies smiling in Dr. Larch's arms.*

LARCH (*V.O.*)

In truth, we've only ever had one real *problem*.

We close in on the infant until his face fills the screen.

LARCH (*V.O.*)

His name was Homer Wells.

Dr. Larch hands over the infant to the adopting parents.

LARCH

I named him after the Greek writer. You know Homer, of course?

Hesitant nods. (They don't look as if they read.)

LARCH *(cont.)*

I made his name "Wells" because I could tell he was very deep.

The parents look with pride at their adopted son.

LARCH (*V.O.*)

In truth, Nurse Angela named him—her father *drilled* wells, and "Homer" was one of her family's umpteen cats.

INT. / EXT. ORPHANAGE—DAY

At the front door, Larch and the nurses wave and call good-bye to Homer; they close the door.

INT. / EXT. ORPHANAGE—NIGHT

The same door swings open; it's another night. The same couple is bringing Homer back. There is concern in their faces as Nurse Edna lets them in.

INT. BOYS' DIVISION, DOORWAY—NIGHT

Larch is delivering his benediction to the boys.

LARCH

"Good night, you Princes of Maine, you Kings of New England!"

As he turns, he is startled by Nurse Edna, waiting with couple #1 and baby Homer.

ADOPTING MOTHER

There's something wrong with him! He never makes a sound.

Larch looks quickly at Homer.

LARCH (*V.O.*)

He didn't cry enough for them, if you can believe it.

ADOPTING FATHER

Do you think we could have a look at someone a little different?

The mother hands over the baby to Larch. Baby Homer lets out a happy squeal as soon as he's in Larch's arms. The parents stare in disbelief.

LARCH (*V.O.*)

Thus was Homer Wells returned. He was too happy a baby.

EXT. ORPHANAGE—DAY

Angela and Edna call and wave good-bye to a two-year-old Homer, leaving with COUPLE #2. *Larch stands on the porch and watches the family head down the hill.*

LARCH (*V.O.*)

The second family had an unfortunate gift for getting sounds out of Homer.

INT. COUPLE #2's HOME—DAY

Larch bursts into the home of the second couple and lifts a crying and bruised Homer out of his bed. There is rage in Larch's eyes as he looks at the couple.

LARCH (*V.O.*)

The rumor was true. They beat him. He couldn't stop crying.

EXT. HILL, ST. CLOUD'S—DAY

Larch carries Homer up the orphanage hill.

LARCH (*V.O.*)

Here in St. Cloud's, I try to consider, with each rule I make or break, that my first priority is an orphan's future.

INT. DELIVERY ROOM—DAY

The naked belly of a VERY PREGNANT WOMAN.

LARCH (*V.O.*)

Easier said than done.

A tiny hand comes in with a stethoscope and puts it on the big belly. Young Homer's head, with the stethoscope around his neck, pops up behind the belly; he closes his eyes as he concentrates on listening to the sounds of the unborn child. Larch stops in the doorway, catching sight of Homer. He smiles faintly.

EXT. COUPLE #3's HOME—DAY

The door opens to a THIRD COUPLE *smiling at us, welcoming and embracing a sixteen-year-old Homer. Behind them waits the would-be* STEPSISTER—*an attractive girl, a little older than Homer.*

LARCH (*V.O.*)

I told the third family to take good care—this was a special boy.

INT. STEPSISTER'S BEDROOM—NIGHT

Homer and the stepsister are in bed together. The parents burst in on them—the father chasing Homer around and around the bed, the mother beating her daughter, who covers herself with a pillow.

LARCH (*V.O.*)

It was Homer who took too much good care of himself.

EXT. COUPLE #3's HOME—NIGHT

From her window, the stepsister watches Homer leave the house carrying his suitcase. Homer looks up at her as he walks quickly to the street.

EXT. ORPHANAGE—EARLY MORNING

It's after dawn, but still a little dark, as Homer walks to the orphanage door, suitcase in hand. A HUGELY PREGNANT WOMAN *arrives at the same time. They stand awkwardly next to each other, waiting for someone to answer the door. The woman is crying. Homer reaches out and takes her hand.*

HOMER

Don't be frightened. Everyone is nice here.

PREGNANT WOMAN

Do you live here?

HOMER

I just belong here.

The woman sniffles; she nods vaguely. The door opens. Nurse Edna lets the woman in and embraces Homer.

LARCH (*V.O.*)

What could I do with him? He kept coming back!

INT. LARCH'S OFFICE—DAY

Larch instructs an older Homer from Gray's Anatomy. *Homer is bored and looks out the window.*

LARCH

Homer, if you're going to stay at St. Cloud's, I expect you to be of use.

INT. DELIVERY ROOM—DAY

Homer looks adoringly at Dr. Larch as Larch examines ANOTHER PREGNANT WOMAN. *Larch waves Homer over; he places the boy's hand on the woman's abdomen, to feel the fetus kicking.*

LARCH (*V.O.*)

But, in failing to withhold love, had I created a true and everlasting orphan? I had been too successful with Homer Wells. I had managed to make the orphanage his *home.*

INT. OPERATING ROOM—DAY

Larch closes a door quickly behind him (so that Homer doesn't see the ABORTION PATIENT *in the O.R.).*

INT. DELIVERY ROOM—DAY

Homer assists Larch in delivering a BABY.

EXT. INCINERATOR—DAY

Homer carries a white enamel pail to the incinerator. He looks inside the pail; he stops.

LARCH (*V.O.*)

God forgive me. I have *made* an orphan by loving him too much. Homer Wells will belong to St. Cloud's, forever.

Hold on Homer's disgusted expression as he stares at the contents of the pail.

END TITLE SEQUENCE. FADE OUT. We hear a song playing on an old phonograph.

INT. DISPENSARY—DAY

We see the song playing on the old phonograph. Dr. Larch is taking ether. He holds the bottle in one hand, the cone over his mouth and nose with his other hand.

SUPER: ST. CLOUD'S, MAINE, MARCH 1943.

When Larch dozes off, his hand loosens its grip on the cone; the cone falls off his face, and he wakes up. Then he puts the cone back in place, dripping more ether from the bottle to the gauze covering the cone.

Pan the dispensary, which also serves as Larch's photo gallery and bedroom-apartment. The ether-bed is separated from the room by a hospital curtain (the kind on casters). We see the recording revolving, the glass-encased cabinets of medical supplies, the old photographs of St. Cloud's.

Homer enters; he stands uncomfortably, watching Larch for a moment. Then he turns around and walks back into the corridor.

INT. CORRIDOR—DAY

Homer calls out as though he's just coming down the corridor.

HOMER

Dr. Larch! Dr. Larch!

INT. DISPENSARY—DAY

Larch wakes up; he shakes off the ether haze. Homer reenters.

HOMER

We've got two new patients, one to deliver.

Dr. Larch and Homer leave together.

INT. CORRIDOR—DAY

The two *doctors walk briskly down the hall, a couple of professionals.*

LARCH

First pregnancy?

HOMER

Yes, for both.

LARCH

(*sarcastically*)

I presume you'd prefer handling the delivery.

HOMER

(*tiredly; an old topic*)

All I said was, I don't want to perform abortions. I have no argument with *you* performing them.

LARCH

You know *how* to help these women—how can you not feel *obligated* to help them when they can't get help anywhere else?

HOMER

One: it's illegal. Two: I didn't ask how to do it—you just showed me.

LARCH

What *else* could I have shown you, Homer? The only thing I can teach you is what I know! In every life, you've got to be of use.

Homer and Larch split off and disappear into two different operating rooms. As he goes, Homer mumbles to himself, "Of use, of use, of use."

INT. OPERATING ROOM—DAY

Larch and Angela are preparing the ether for DOROTHY, *a not visibly pregnant woman. The sounds of labor across the hall can be heard Over.*

LARCH

(holds the cone)

Have you ever had ether, Dorothy?

DOROTHY

Once, when they took out my appendix.

ANGELA

(looks for scar)

No one's touched your appendix.

DOROTHY

Whatever it was . . . the ether made me sick.

LARCH

It won't make you sick this time, Dorothy—not the way I do it, just a drop at a time.

DOROTHY

I can't pay for this, you know—I got no money.

LARCH

One day, Dorothy, if you have any money, a donation to the orphanage would be very much appreciated.

ANGELA

Only if you can afford it.

LARCH

(holds the ether bottle)

Try to think of nothing, Dorothy.

Angela puts the cone over Dorothy's mouth and nose; Larch drips the ether on the cone. A newborn wails in the other O.R. Over.

INT. DELIVERY ROOM—DAY

Homer has delivered CARLA. *A newborn baby is screaming in Edna's arms. Homer is attending to Carla, who is panting.*

HOMER

That was good, Carla—that was *perfect*. Everything's fine.

CARLA

I don't wanna see it!

EDNA

You don't have to see it, dear. Don't worry.

CARLA

I don't even wanna know what sex it is—don't tell me!

HOMER

We won't tell you, Carla. You're going to be okay.

EDNA

Your *baby's* going to be okay, too.

CARLA

I don't wanna know!

Larch pops into the delivery room; he peers at the baby.

LARCH

He's a big boy!

CARLA

Let me see him, for Christ's sake—I wanna see him.

Edna shows the baby to Carla, who stares, then turns away. Larch whispers to Homer.

LARCH

Would you mind having a look at Dorothy?

INT. OPERATING ROOM—DAY

Angela sits with the still-etherized Dorothy while Larch and Homer confer over a basin containing Dorothy's uterus.

HOMER

There was no visible wound?

LARCH

No. The fetus was dead. Her uterus was virtually *disintegrating*—my stitches pulled right through the tissue!

HOMER

(*mystified*)
It looks like scurvy.

LARCH

(*derisively sarcastic*)
Scurvy! Ah yes, the curse of the old-time sailor, suffering long periods at sea with no fresh fruits or vegetables. Homer, Dorothy isn't a *sailor*!

ANGELA

She's a prostitute, isn't she?

HOMER

(to Angela)

Did you look in her purse?

LARCH

(frustrated)

I looked everywhere else!

Angela hands Larch a bottle of brown liquid.

ANGELA

It's called French Lunar Solution.

Larch wrinkles his nose at the odor.

LARCH

It's not ergot, it's not pituitary extract, it's not oil of rue . . .

ANGELA

It claims to restore monthly regularity.

HOMER

It's obviously an aborticide.

LARCH

Obviously.

Larch wets his finger with the stuff, then touches it to his tongue.

LARCH *(cont.)*

(spits)

Christ, it's oil of tansy!

HOMER

I don't know it.

LARCH

If you take enough of it, your intestines lose their ability to absorb Vitamin C.

HOMER

In other words, scurvy.

LARCH

Good boy. Good job. And you call yourself "not a doctor"!
(to Angela)
Keep an eye on her—she's in trouble.

As Homer turns to leave, Larch stops him; he points to the basin.

LARCH *(cont.)*

Take care of that, will you?

Homer stops, annoyed; he picks up the basin and empties the contents into a white enamel pail.

INT. DINING HALL—AFTERNOON

MISS TITCOMB *is teaching math to some distracted boys and girls in a corner of the dining toom. A blackboard on wheels is a mass of numbers. Homer, passing through the dining toom with the white enamel pail, attracts the attention of* BUSTER, *a sixteen-year-old who is picking over a plate of pastries on a table. Buster immediately goes with Homer.*

BUSTER

I'll help you.

Homer shakes his head, keeps walking. Buster follows. Dr. Larch passes close to Buster. Buster makes a face, disgusted.

EXT. INCINERATOR—AFTERNOON

Buster and Homer tramp through the snow toward the incinerator. Homer still carries the pail.

BUSTER

He *sniffs* that ether! I've seen him do it!

HOMER

It's because he's too tired to sleep. He has to.

BUSTER

He *smells* like he could put you to sleep!

HOMER

He's a doctor, Buster—doctors smell like ether.

BUSTER

You're a doctor, Homer—you don't smell like ether.

HOMER

I'm *not* a doctor. I haven't been to medical school—I haven't even been to high school!

BUSTER

But you've studied with the old man for *years*!

HOMER

I'm *not* a doctor!

BUSTER

I'm sorry, Homer.

Buster stands watching as Homer empties the pail into the incinerator.

INT. DISPENSARY—NIGHT

With his head inclined to the giant ear of Larch's phonograph, FUZZY*—six, thin, and pale, and looking remarkably like an embryo—is listening to a recording. He can't hear what Larch and Homer are saying about him as they construct a humidified tent over a small hospital bed on wheels. The humidifier is operated by a car battery.*

LARCH

Fuzzy is not uncommon. I tell you, there's something about the premature babies of alcoholic mothers. They seem susceptible to every damn thing that comes along.

HOMER

I haven't read that.

LARCH

I haven't, either. But you *will*. The morons who write the books should do a little research *here*.

HOMER

But isn't Fuzzy just . . . well, underdeveloped?

LARCH

When *doesn't* he have bronchitis? I wouldn't call his bronchial infections "underdeveloped." Would you?

Larch plucks Fuzzy from in front of the phonograph and zips him into the breathing tent. Fuzzy smiles. As Larch leaves, MARY AGNES, *a pretty but tough-looking teenager, comes into the dispensary.*

HOMER

What is it, Mary Agnes?

Mary Agnes smiles at Homer; then she sticks her tongue out at him. Homer looks at her impassively, but as the moment continues his expression suggests his annoyance. Fuzzy starts to cough; he wheezes as he breathes. Homer leans down; he peers at Fuzzy through a hole by the zipper of the tent.

MARY AGNES

(garbled because of her tongue)

Look!

Homer examines Mary Agnes's tongue.

HOMER

Did you bite it?

MARY AGNES

I don't remember.

HOMER

(dismissively)

It looks like you bit it—it'll be all right.

MARY AGNES

Maybe I was kissing someone and he bit me.

HOMER

(looks at her tongue again)

No, you did it yourself. Maybe in your sleep.

MARY AGNES

I must have been *dreaming* of kissing someone.

Homer is not responding to her come-on. He wheels Fuzzy into the hall.

HOMER

Story time, Fuzzy!

INT. GIRLS' DIVISION—NIGHT

In the girls' bunk room, Nurse Edna is saying prayers. The girls lie with their palms pressed together on their chests.

EDNA

"Oh Lord, support us all the day long . . ."

EXT. ST. CLOUD'S—THE HILL—NIGHT

The building of St. Cloud's is silhouetted against the sky. Carla, the woman we saw deliver the baby, is heading down the hill alone; she sobs, not looking back.

EDNA (*O.S.*)

". . . until the shadows lengthen and the evening comes, and the busy world is hushed, and the fever of life is over, and our work is done."

INT. GIRLS' DIVISION—NIGHT

In the bunk room again, with Edna and the girls.

EDNA

"Then in Thy mercy grant us safe lodging, and holy rest, and peace at the last."

ALL THE GIRLS

Amen! Amen! Amen!

INT. BOYS' DIVISION—NIGHT

Dr. Larch is reading from Oliver Twist*—the death scene of Bill Sikes's dog. The boys listen in horror in their beds.*

LARCH

"A dog, which had lain concealed till now, ran backwards and forwards on the parapet with a dismal howl, and collecting himself for a spring, jumped for the dead man's shoulders."

Homer enters; he walks quietly to his bed in the far corner of the room, where he starts to undress.

LARCH *(cont.)*

"Missing his aim, he fell into a ditch, turning completely

over as he went; and striking his head against a stone, dashed out his brains."

Larch turns out the lights. From the open doorway to the hall, Larch delivers his nightly benediction.

LARCH *(cont.)*

Good night, you Princes of Maine! You Kings of New England!

Larch closes the door, leaving them in the semidarkness. One young boy runs into Homer's bed, nervously giggling.

FUZZY

(in his breathing tent)

Why does Dr. Larch *do* that every night?

CURLY

(about seven)

Maybe to scare us . . .

COPPERFIELD

(about eleven)

No, you jerk.

STEERFORTH

(about nine)
Dr. Larch *loves* us!

FUZZY

But why does he do *that*?

BUSTER

He does it because we like it.

The boys silently agree, Homer among them.

EXT. ST. CLOUD'S—EARLY MORNING

The girls, led by Mary Agnes, round a corner of the orphanage, towing a sled piled high with snowballs.

MARY AGNES

Buster is mine. You two get Copperfield and Curly. Nobody touches Fuzzy.

They shriek as the boys suddenly surprise them. Buster throws two hard snowballs that hit Mary Agnes and CLARA *(eight or nine) before Mary Agnes overwhelms him and repeatedly sticks his head in the snow. Copperfield, terrified of Mary Agnes, escapes. Curly misses, then tips over the sled of snowballs as*

Clara and the adorable HAZEL *(five or six) throw him to the ground. Fuzzy drops his one snowball; he runs aimlessly in circles, coughing, as Nurse Edna explodes from a door of the orphanage.*

EDNA

Stop it! No fighting! *Share* the snowballs!

BUSTER

(mouth full of snow)
They're *our* snowballs! They *stole* them!

MARY AGNES

They attacked us—just like the Japs!

Fuzzy coughs and wheezes, trying to catch his breath.

EDNA

Listen to you, Fuzzy! You've been running. You get to the shower!

A NEW COUPLE *comes up the hill. The orphans stop and stare, brushing snow off themselves, struggling to make themselves look presentable. Curly is desperate to look his best. Mary Agnes doesn't bother to pretty herself. She whispers to Clara and Hazel.*

MARY AGNES

I know the type—they'll take one of the babies.

INT. DINING HALL—MORNING

The children are eating breakfast as the would-be parents walk around the tables, looking over the assembled orphans. Curly works on his table manners; he forks and eats a piece of a pancake with elegance. Angela and Edna try to make the couple slow down by the older children, but the couple stop and stare at the adorable Hazel.

INT. BABY ROOM—MORNING

Larch and Homer are examining the babies. The doctors are checking the babies' grips, their eyes, ears, and throats.

Angela appears in the doorway.

ANGELA

Wilbur, the adopting couple is waiting in your office.

LARCH

(*irritated*)

Life is waiting.

Angela disappears. Larch looks at the next baby's record (attached to the bed).

LARCH (*cont.*)

Where's the name sheet?

HOMER

Nobody's named this one yet.

LARCH

It's my turn!

Homer is tired of this game. Larch touches the child's forehead with his index finger.

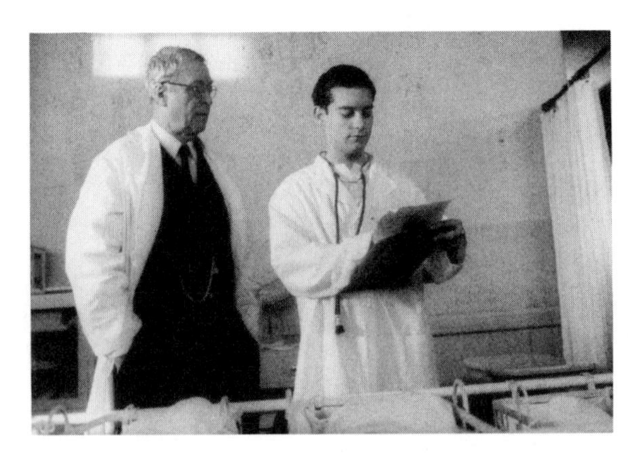

LARCH *(cont.)*

Henceforth you shall be . . . Little Dorrit!

The baby starts to cry.

HOMER

He doesn't like it.
(looks at the record)
He's a boy. That's why.

LARCH

Can't a boy be a Dorrit?

HOMER

I don't think so.

LARCH

You do it then.

Homer points his finger at the child's forehead like a gun.

HOMER

Henceforth you shall be . . . Little Wilbur.

LARCH

I'm not crazy about the "Little . . ."

Homer is writing the name.

HOMER

Okay, he's just a Wilbur then.

LARCH

We haven't had a Wilbur here in a year or so, have we?
We used to have *dozens*!

They are interrupted by Copperfield, who comes running from the corridor.

COPPERFIELD

They picked Hazel! The idiots chose Hazel!

INT. GIRLS' DIVISION—DAY

Hazel is being fussed over by Edna. Hazel clutches a cardboard suitcase and a tattered rag doll. Mary Agnes, by far the oldest, sits on a bed.

MARY AGNES

If people want to adopt one of us, they should have to take the oldest first.

EDNA

Please, Mary Agnes! This is Hazel's special day—don't make her feel sad.

MARY AGNES

Hazel's practically the youngest of us. She should be the *last* to leave!

CLARA

At least Hazel can talk. Usually they take one of the stupid babies.

MARY AGNES

They take the babies so they won't ever have to tell them that they were orphans!

HAZEL

(begins to cry)
I'm not a baby!

MARY AGNES

If you cry, Hazel, they'll just send you back.

EDNA

Mary Agnes, that's not true!

Hazel cries harder.

MARY AGNES

That's what they did to me!

EDNA

You *wanted* to come back—that's why you cried.
(to Hazel)
You can cry if you feel like it, Hazel. You cry as much as you want to.

INT. LARCH'S OFFICE—DAY

Homer is in the corridor outside the office, overhearing Larch's lecture to the couple adopting Hazel.

LARCH

It is strictly for our orphans' sake that I destroy any records of their natural mothers. Of course they will, one day, want to know. But orphans, especially, should look forward to their *futures*. Not back to their pasts.

INT. WINDOW, CORRIDOR—DAY

Homer sees Curly standing all alone by a window in the corridor; a suitcase is next to him.

HOMER

Hi, Curly. You going somewhere?

Curly shakes his head.

CURLY

I thought they might take me.

HOMER

They wanted a girl.

CURLY

Nobody ever wants me!

Homer embraces Curly and lifts him up; he grabs the suitcase and continues down the corridor.

HOMER

You're one of the best, Curly—we wouldn't let just anyone take you.

CURLY

Dr. Larch wouldn't let just anyone take *any* of us!

HOMER

That's true.

CURLY

Nobody's asked for me, have they?

HOMER

Nobody special enough, Curly.

CURLY

You mean somebody asked?

HOMER

Only the right people can have you, Curly.

Homer disappears into the boys' bunk room carrying Curly and his suitcase, leaving the corridor empty.

INT./EXT. ORPHANAGE—DAY

Faces in the windows: the orphans watch Hazel walking across the snowy lawn with her new parents.

INT. GIRLS' DIVISION—NIGHT

Edna (with the girls) gives her good-bye blessing to Hazel.

EDNA

Let us be happy for Hazel. Hazel has found a family. Good night, Hazel.

THE GIRLS

Good night, Hazel! Good night, Hazel! Good night, Hazel!

INT./EXT. ORPHANAGE—FRONT DOOR—DAY

The front door opens. The orphans excitedly run outside onto the green lawn, into the warm weather of spring.

INT. DISPENSARY—MORNING

Angela is singing along with the song on the phonograph, a more romantic song than before, which rouses Larch from his ether. He is grumpy, but she sings the song in his ear and won't give him back the ether cone; he rolls away from her, but she tickles him and bites his ear, coaxing him into a more playful mood.

LARCH

I was dreaming about you. How beautiful you were!

ANGELA

You weren't dreaming about me.

LARCH

I was!

Playfully, she slips out of his embrace.

ANGELA

Then I wasn't beautiful.

LARCH

You were! You *are*! It was fantastic.

ANGELA

It was just the ether, Wilbur . . .

INT. HOSPITAL ROOM—NIGHT

Homer wheels a tray with glasses of water between the beds. A DISTRAUGHT PREGNANT WOMAN *stops him by her bed.*

HOMER

Are you okay? Can I get you anything?

DISTRAUGHT WOMAN

No one but me ever put a hand on me, to feel that baby. Don't you want to touch it or put your ear down to it?

HOMER

Okay.

Homer touches the woman's belly.

DISTRAUGHT WOMAN

Put your ear there. Go on.

Homer cautiously lays his ear against her belly.

DISTRAUGHT WOMAN *(cont.)*

You shouldn't have a baby if there's no one who wants to put his face right there!

She holds Homer's head against her belly; she presses his face into her. She shuts her eyes. Homer's eyes stare widely. Dr. Larch stops in the doorway; he watches with concern.

DISTRAUGHT WOMAN *(cont.)*

Stay right there. Right where you are. Stay right here. Right here.

EXT. ST. CLOUD'S—TRAIN STATION—DAY

Homer at the train station, staring down the empty tracks. Buster is hanging around with him, kicking a rock.

BUSTER

Do you ever think about leaving this place to go find them?

Homer makes no response. As the train approaches, Homer and Buster go sit on a loading cart. They see the distraught woman (no longer pregnant) from Homer's experience of a few nights ago; she is leaving St. Cloud's without her baby, waiting for the approaching train. Her face is a mask. The DISAPPROVING STATIONMASTER *gives her a hard look.*

BUSTER *(cont.)*

I mean your parents.

HOMER

I know who you mean. I think about leaving here, but not to find *them*.

BUSTER

Why not?

HOMER

Whoever they were, they didn't *do* any of the things parents are supposed to do. Dr. Larch did those things, and Nurse Edna, and Nurse Angela.

BUSTER

Yeah. But sometimes I wish I could meet mine, anyway.

HOMER

What for, Buster? What would you do if you met them?

BUSTER

Uh . . . I'd like to show them that I can cook, a little.

HOMER

You cook very well!

BUSTER

And that I can drive a truck!

HOMER

(laughing)
Better than I can!

BUSTER

Sometimes I want to meet them so I can kill them. Just sometimes.

Buster is ashamed; he knows he's said the wrong thing.

BUSTER *(cont.)*

Homer, you know I would never kill anyone—you know I wouldn't.

HOMER

I know.

The slowly moving train has stopped. There are SOLDIERS leaning out the windows. Buster turns to see Mary Agnes walking past the train—she's doing her best to look grown-up, sophisticated. One of the soldiers reaches out and gently tugs on her hair. Mary Agnes is enraged; she spits at the soldier.

BUSTER

I think Mary Agnes could kill someone.

HOMER

I doubt it. She's just an . . .

Mary Agnes spits at all *the soldiers.*

HOMER *(cont.)*

. . . emotional girl.

The soldiers roll up the windows as Mary Agnes improvises some verbal abuse.

BUSTER

What's she so emotional about?

HOMER

(shrugs)

I don't know. She got left here, like the rest of us, didn't she?

Camera closes on Homer.

INT. DINING HALL—NIGHT

The orphans are watching King Kong, *the part when the giant ape first captures the screaming Fay Wray. Intercut* Kong *with the orphans' rapt faces. Homer sits near the front, mesmerized by the film. Dr. Larch and Angela sit by the projector; Larch is reading a letter. Fuzzy points to the screen.*

FUZZY

(coughing)

He thinks she's his *mother!*

King Kong is undressing Fay Wray in the cave.

COPPERFIELD

He doesn't think she's his mother, Fuzzy.

FUZZY

He does so! He *loves* her!

CLARA

How could she be his *mother?*

Larch shakes the letter in front of Angela.

LARCH

(a harsh whisper)

They want to replace me! The Board of Trustees wants to *replace* me!

ANGELA

(whispering back)

They just want you to hire some new help.

LARCH

Some new *things* would be useful. I don't need any "new help."

The film breaks—to huge cries of disappointment from the orphans. Fuzzy coughs and coughs while Larch fumbles with the projector. Angela turns on the light while Larch squints at the broken film. The orphans are chanting, "Kong! Kong!"

LARCH *(cont.)*

Homer! I need you!

Homer gets up and walks to the projector.

LARCH *(cont.)*

I thought you took care of this. It always breaks in the same place. It's your splice, isn't it?

HOMER

(angry)

It's *your* splice! You blame me for everything!

Larch abruptly lets go of the film.

LARCH

Angela, we need a new movie, a new projector, a new typewriter—*that's* what they should replace around here!

Edna comes in; she speaks to Larch, then quickly leaves.

EDNA

We have a delivery. Imminent, in my estimation . . .

Larch turns to Homer.

LARCH

Homer, would you get this one?

Homer shifts his weight to the other foot, aggravated; he stands there.

HOMER

She's a patient, right? She should see a doctor.

Homer and Larch stare at each other.

LARCH

(trying to stay calm)

Homer, you are a skilled and gifted surgeon. You have near-perfect obstetrical and gynecological procedure.

Homer is also trying to avoid a fight.

HOMER

I just mean I'd rather fix the movie. Tonight.

Larch can't hide his disappointment.

LARCH

Sure. Okay. You splice. I'll deliver.

It is an uneasy peace.

INT. BOYS' DIVISION—NIGHT (LATER)

Homer is adjusting Fuzzy's breathing tent as the other boys climb into bed.

FUZZY

Homer . . . doesn't King Kong think the woman is his *mother?*

HOMER

Uh, sure—that's what Kong thinks, all right.

FUZZY

That's why Kong loves her!

Larch comes in and walks over to Homer and Fuzzy. Larch and Homer exchange a look.

HOMER

I thought it was my turn.

LARCH

It is. I'll get this. You go ahead.

Homer sits down with David Copperfield. *There is quiet anticipation while Homer readies himself to read.*

HOMER

(*reading*)
"Whether I shall turn out to be the hero of my own life, or whether that station will be held by anybody else, these pages must show."

Larch continues to adjust Fuzzy's breathing tent.

HOMER (*cont.*)

"I was a posthumous child. My father's eyes had closed upon the light of this world six months, when mine opened on it."

FUZZY

(*whispers to Larch*)
His father's dead, right?

LARCH

(*whispering back*)
That's right, Fuzz.

Close on Fuzzy.

HOMER (*O.S.*)

(*continues reading*)
"There is something strange to me, even now, in the reflection that he never saw me . . ."

As Larch bends over Fuzzy to fix the breathing apparatus, Fuzzy whispers.

FUZZY

Is *your* father dead?

LARCH

(*nods, whispers*)
Cirrhosis—it's a disease of the liver.

FUZZY

Liver killed him?

LARCH

Alcohol killed him—he drank himself to death.

FUZZY

But did you know him?

LARCH

Barely. It hardly mattered that I knew him.

FUZZY

Did you know your mother better?

LARCH

(*nods, still whispers*)
She's dead now, too. She was a nanny.

FUZZY

What's a nanny do?

LARCH

She looks after other people's children.

FUZZY

Did you grow up around here?

LARCH

No. She was an immigrant.

FUZZY

What's an immigrant?

LARCH

Someone not from Maine.

EXT. ST. CLOUD'S—NIGHT

The orphanage in moonlight. Not a sound.

EXT. ST. CLOUD'S—MORNING

The children are chasing a ball near the incinerator.

A VERY FRIGHTENED GIRL—*not one of the orphans*—is *lying next to the incinerator.*

Edna kneels by the strange girl, who cringes with fear.

EDNA

No one's going to hurt you, dear. Have you come to visit us? We have beds, you know. Have you had any breakfast? What's your name?

The girl won't speak; when Edna touches the girl's forehead, she pulls back her hand in alarm.

INT. OPERATING ROOM—MORNING

Edna is holding the head of the frightened young girl. The girl is feverishly hot and whimpering; she keeps looking at her feet in the stirrups as if she's an animal caught in a trap. Larch and Homer stand on either side of her.

EDNA

Her temperature is a hundred and four.

LARCH

(very gently)
How old are you, dear? Thirteen?

The girl shakes her head. The pain stabs her again.

LARCH *(cont.)*

Twelve? Are you twelve, dear?
(the girl nods)
You have to tell me how long you've been pregnant.
(the girl freezes)
Three months?

Another stab of pain contorts the girl.

LARCH *(cont.)*

Are you *four* months pregnant?

The girl holds her breath while he examines her abdomen; Homer very delicately examines the girl's abdomen, too.

HOMER

(whispers to Larch)
She's at least *five*.

The girl goes rigid as Larch bends into position.

LARCH

Dear child, it won't hurt when I look. I'm just going to *look*.

Homer assists Larch with the speculum.

LARCH *(cont.)*

Tell me: you haven't done something to yourself, have you?

TWELVE-YEAR-OLD GIRL

It wasn't me!

LARCH

Did you go to someone else?

TWELVE-YEAR-OLD GIRL

He said he was a doctor. I would never have stuck that inside me!

HOMER

Stuck *what* inside you?

TWELVE-YEAR-OLD GIRL

It wasn't me!

Homer holds the girl still—she is babbling on and on while Larch is examining her.

TWELVE-YEAR-OLD GIRL *(cont.)*

It wasn't me! I would never do no such thing! I wouldn't stick that inside me! It wasn't me!

Larch, his wild eye peering into the speculum, makes an audible gasp from the shock of what he sees inside the girl. Larch tells Homer to have a look. Larch then whispers something to Edna; she brings the ether bottle and cone quickly. Larch starts putting the cone in place, over the nose and mouth of the frightened girl. Homer bends to the speculum.

LARCH

(to the twelve-year-old)

Listen, you've been very brave. I'm going to put you to sleep—you won't feel it anymore. You've been brave enough.

Homer stares into the speculum; he closes his eyes. The girl is resisting the ether, but her eyelids flutter closed.

EDNA

That's a heavy sedation.

LARCH

You *bet* it's a heavy sedation! The fetus is unexpelled, her uterus is punctured, she has acute peritonitis, and there's a foreign object. I think it's a crochet hook.

Homer has pulled off his surgical mask. He leans over the scrub sink, splashing cold water on his face.

LARCH *(cont.)*

(to Homer)
If she'd come to you four months ago and asked you for a simple D and C, what would you have decided to do? *Nothing? This* is what doing nothing gets you, Homer. It means that someone else is going to do the job—some moron who doesn't know *how*!

Homer, furious, leaves the operating room. Edna lifts the girl's eyelids for Larch so that he can see how well under the ether she is.

LARCH *(cont.)*

I wish you'd come to *me*, dear child. You should have come to me, instead.

INT. CORRIDOR—MORNING

Homer storms down the hall, then stops, pulling off his white coat. Angry, pacing, he kicks at nothing.

EXT. ST. CLOUD'S—GRAVEYARD—EARLY MORNING

Buster and Homer are digging the pit. Larch paces by the coffin of the 12-year-old girl.

BUSTER

What'd she die of?

LARCH

(inhales deeply)
She died of *secrecy*, she died of *ignorance* . . .

Buster nods, but he's totally bewildered.

LARCH *(cont.)*

(to Homer)

If you expect people to be responsible for their children, you have to give them the right to decide whether or not to *have* children. Wouldn't you agree?

Buster doesn't get it. Homer has heard this too many times; he rolls his eyes.

HOMER

How about expecting people to be responsible enough to control themselves to begin with?

LARCH

How about this child? You expect *her* to be responsible?

Homer looks away.

HOMER

I didn't mean her. I'm talking about . . . adults.

(annoyed)

You know who I mean!

Larch studies him.

EXT./INT. ST. CLOUD'S ROAD—TRUCK CAB—DAY

Buster is driving the old pickup truck, with the shovels and a wheelbarrow in the back. Larch and Homer are in the cab; they are being bounced all over the cab by Buster's wild driving. Larch looks at Homer; he stares at him with a curious smile.

HOMER

What?!

Larch says nothing. Homer gives him a look.

LARCH

(smiling)
It's just a marvel to me that you still have such high expectations of people.

HOMER

I'm happy I amuse you.

LARCH

(to Homer)
Try to look at it this way. What choice does Buster have? What are his options? Nobody will ever adopt him.
(Buster considers this)

HOMER

Try to look at it *this* way. Buster and I are sitting right here beside you. We could have ended up in the incinerator!
(Buster grins)

LARCH

Happy to be alive, under any circumstances—is that your point?

Buster is distracted; he drives the truck into a ditch and it bounces around, missing a tree by an inch. He is up on the road again in a few seconds.

HOMER

Happy to be alive . . . I guess so.

They are all distracted by a luxurious convertible that overtakes them on the hill to the orphanage. The fast car is driven by a handsome man in the uniform of the Army Air Corps—a YOUNG OFFICER. *From the passenger seat, a* BEAUTIFUL YOUNG WOMAN *smiles at them, rendering them speechless.*

EXT. ORPHANAGE DRIVEWAY—DAY

The luxurious convertible (now parked) has drawn all the orphans to it. The handsome young officer (WALLY) *and the beautiful young woman* (CANDY) *stand confused by the car; they are surrounded by the curious orphans, with whom they are painfully self-conscious. They are as overly friendly to the children as they are anxious of Larch and Homer and Buster (in their gravedigging attire), who are getting out of the truck. Nervously, Wally gives the children chocolates.*

CANDY

So many children. Are they all orphans?

WALLY

Well, this *is* an orphanage.

The kids climb into Wally's car.

CANDY

Oh, they're getting into the car . . . watch your fingers!

Curly tugs on Candy's dress, staring up at her, his face already smeared with chocolate.

CURLY

I'm the best.

CANDY

(*sweetly*)
You are?

WALLY

(*good with kids*)
The best? Wow! The best at *what?*

CURLY

I'm the best one.

Curly's nose is streaming snot. Candy kneels beside him and holds her handkerchief to his nose.

CANDY

Here, blow . . .

Curly tries to talk while she's holding his nose.

CURLY

I really *am* the best, I just have a cold.

CANDY

Blow! There, I bet that feels better.

CURLY

(*sniffs*)
Yeah.

The other orphans are dying with envy—Candy is so beautiful. (Some, like Buster, are torn between Candy and the car.)

LARCH

Curly, come here!

CURLY

(*to Larch*)
Tell them! I'm the one.

Virtually all the orphans have climbed into Wally's car.

HOMER

(*to Wally*)

I'm sorry. They're not used to seeing a car like this.

WALLY

It's okay—I don't mind.

Larch, scowling, presents himself to the new couple.

WALLY *(cont.)*

We brought some chocolates for the kids.

LARCH

(*witheringly*)

Chocolates. How *thoughtful.*

Larch picks up Curly and carries him toward the boys' division.

CURLY

I'm the best! *Tell* them!

LARCH

You're the best, Curly.

INT. LARCH'S OFFICE—DAY

Homer is seated in the desk chair. The impressive couple sit in front of him.

HOMER

So, Mrs. . . .

CANDY

Candy. Candy Kendall.

Wally jumps up to his feet to shake Homer's hand.

WALLY

Wally! Wally Worthington.

Wally sits down. The three sit still for an awkward moment.

HOMER

(to Candy)
How many months are you?

CANDY

(whispers)
Two.

Homer writes on a piece of paper. Candy and Wally exchange a worried look.

WALLY

So, now, uh . . . you're not . . . I mean, do *you* do the—

HOMER

No. Dr. Larch will be performing the procedure.

WALLY

(relieved)
Ah, well . . . okay. Good! I just wondered . . .

Edna pokes her head in the door.

EDNA

Excuse me, Homer. Dr. Larch said this one is your turn.

Edna quickly sees that all three of them have misunderstood her.

EDNA *(cont.)*

Oh, dear—I'm sorry. I meant the circumcision. That boy you delivered on Tuesday . . .

HOMER

Sure. Fine. Have you prepped him?

EDNA

I'll get started.

Candy and Wally can't conceal how impressed they are with the young Homer.

INT. CORRIDOR—DAY

Homer walks down the corridor, dressed in his operating gown, as the door to the O.R. opens and Wally stumbles out, hurriedly opening a window. Wally breathes deeply to regain his composure.

WALLY

I think it was the ether—the smell got to me.
(pause)
God. This is all my fault.

Edna comes down the hall with a dirt-stained, crying Curly who's covering one eye.

EDNA

(over the din)
Steerforth got into the pantry—he's eaten all the pie dough.

CURLY

(sobbing)
He wasn't sharing it, either.

EDNA

He's down the hall, throwing up.

Homer nods to Edna, who is marching off with Curly. Wally smiles at Homer.

HOMER

What kind of plane are you flying?

WALLY

A B-24 Liberator.

HOMER

Liberator . . .

WALLY

Have you enlisted?

HOMER

They wouldn't take me. I'm Class IV—I've got a heart defect.

WALLY

Really! Is it serious?

HOMER

No, it's not serious. I'm just not supposed to get excited. You know—no strain, no stress. I try to keep calm all the time.

Wally hears Homer's facetiousness—how tired he is of his heart condition.

WALLY

Oh, well. I don't imagine there's any strain or stress around *here*!

Homer appreciates the joke.

The door to the operating room that Wally exited opens into the corridor; Candy is being wheeled out on a gurney by Larch and Angela. Wally rushes to Candy's side. Homer follows slowly. Candy is groggy, coming out of the ether.

WALLY *(cont.)*

How is she doing?

LARCH

Just fine.

CANDY

(slurred speech)
Boy or girl?

ANGELA

It was nothing—it's all over.

WALLY

It's all over, honey.

They walk Candy on her gurney. Homer looks after them.

CANDY

(slurred speech)
I would like to have a baby, one day. I really would.

ANGELA

Why, of course—you can have as many children as you want. I'm sure you'll have very beautiful children.

Larch wheels Candy behind a curtain.

LARCH

You'll have Princes of Maine! You'll have Kings of New England!

Larch has a different tone of voice when he speaks to Wally.

LARCH *(cont.)*

I suggest you find yourself some fresh air, Lieutenant.

Wally is left alone in the corridor.

INT. BOYS' DIVISION—DAY

Cranked at three-quarters, Fuzzy sits in bed, wheezing and coughing. He's drawing with great intensity, using crayons on a piece of paper held by a clipboard. Homer sits on the end of Fuzzy's bed, cleaning up Steerforth. Homer pauses to look out the window; he sees Wally, dashing and spotless in his uniform beside his flashy car. A life Homer might have had crosses his face.

FUZZY (*O.S.*)

Homer, when is Halloween?

Homer turns to Fuzzy, who holds up his picture—a big pumpkin with a jack-o-lantern face.

HOMER

(distracted)

Uh . . . it's the end of October.

FUZZY

Is that soon?

Homer looks at Fuzzy; his little body is working hard just to breathe.

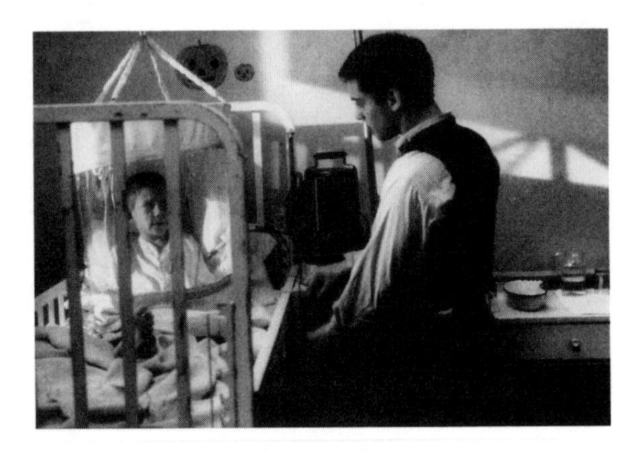

STEERFORTH

That's a few months away, Fuzz.

(to Homer)

I still don't feel so good.

FUZZY

(disappointed)

Oh. It's the best time! How come we only get pumpkins once a year?

Fuzzy coughs and coughs.

HOMER

Don't get too excited, Fuzzy.

FUZZY

Why can't we have pumpkins for Christmas, too? We don't get any good presents at Christmas, anyway.

Homer looks out the window at Wally again. His decision forms.

EXT. ORPHANAGE DRIVEWAY—DAY

Homer approaches the flashy car, where Wally is still pacing.

HOMER

Has anyone offered you anything to eat?

WALLY

Actually, someone did. I just didn't think I could eat anything.

An awkward silence, which Homer covers by examining the car.

HOMER

(trying to sound casual)
I wonder if you might give me a ride.

WALLY

Sure! Be glad to! Uh . . . a ride where?

HOMER

(unprepared)
Where are you going?

WALLY

We're heading back to Cape Kenneth.

Homer nods, but he has no idea where Cape Kenneth is.

HOMER

Cape Kenneth . . .

Wally nods.

HOMER *(cont.)*

That sounds fine.

INT. STAIRWAY/CORRIDOR—DAY

Homer runs up the stairs, two steps at a time; he races into a corridor at full speed, exhilarated. Suddenly Dr. Larch appears in front of him. Homer stops abruptly, out of breath, unable to speak.

INT. LARCH'S OFFICE—DAY

As Homer stands guiltily, Larch rifles through an X-ray file, holding various X rays up to the lit screen. He quickly finds the one he's looking for, attaching it briefly to the screen for a confirming look—a heart X ray, which Larch waves at Homer as he talks.

LARCH

(sarcastic)
Doubtless you'll let me know what immensely worthwhile or at least *useful* thing it is that you find to do.

HOMER

(restrained)
I wasn't intending to leave here in order to be entirely useless—I expect I'll find some ways to be of use.

LARCH

In other parts of the world, I suppose there are other ways.

HOMER

(still restrained)
Of course.

LARCH

(blows up)
Are you really so *stupid* that you imagine you're going to find a more gratifying life? What you're going to find is people like the poor people who get left here—only nobody takes care of them half as well! And you won't be able to take care of them, either. There's no taking care of *anybody*—not out there!

HOMER

(feeling trapped)
You know I'm grateful for everything you've done for me . . .

LARCH

(calmly)
I don't need your gratitude.

Larch hands Homer the heart X ray.

HOMER

(exasperated)
I don't need this—I know all about my condition!

LARCH

It's your heart—you ought to take it with you.

Camera closes on Homer with the X ray.

INT. KITCHEN—LATE AFTERNOON

Buster and Mary Agnes are serving the evening meal while Larch rails at Angela and Edna, who are helping Buster and Mary Agnes. The sound of children in the dining hall is intermittent and chaotic.

EDNA

Going where? Does he have a plan of some kind?

ANGELA

Will he be back soon?

LARCH

I don't know! He's just leaving—
(to Angela)
you're the one who says he needs to see the world!
(to Edna)
That's what he'll do—he'll see the world!

EDNA

(stunned)
He's leaving . . .

ANGELA

He'll need clothes . . . some money . . .

LARCH

Let him try to *make* some money! That's part of "seeing the world," isn't it?

ANGELA

(angrily)

Oh, just stop it! You knew this was going to happen. He's a young man.

LARCH

(almost breaking)

He's still a boy—out in the world, he's still a boy.

ANGELA

(with sympathy)

Just find him some clothes, Wilbur. He could use some clothes.

Camera closes on Larch, fighting tears.

INT. BOYS' DIVISION—AFTERNOON

Homer is packing his things—we see the heart X ray, and some photos of Larch and Edna and Angela.

Larch approaches Homer with a small bundle of clothes.

LARCH

(gently, almost reverently)

I think these will fit you.

Homer is grateful and ashamed. Before he can speak, Edna is there—a wad of bills in her hand. She tries to put the money in his pocket; when he refuses it, she simply puts the money in his open suitcase, stuffing the bills under his clothes.

EDNA

You'll need some money—just a little something, until you find a job.

Larch and Edna retreat from him, humbly, as if they were his servants.

EXT. DRIVEWAY—AFTERNOON

As Homer puts his stuff in the trunk of Wally's car, Angela can't resist touching his face. She is too upset to speak.

From a window, Larch is watching the departure. He sees Homer saying good-bye to the children, embracing them.

From another window, Fuzzy just stares. (Of course he's coughing.)

We see Wally carrying Candy to the car.

CANDY

(groggy)
I'm okay—I can walk.

WALLY

I don't want you to walk—I want to carry you. Should I put the top up? It might get cold.

CANDY

No—keep it down. I want to feel the air.

She speaks to Homer, touching his sleeve, like a sleepy person, as Wally puts her gently in the backseat.

CANDY *(cont.)*

(still groggy)
Coming with us? It's always a good idea to have a doctor along for the ride.

Homer gets in the passenger seat beside Wally, who starts the car; suddenly there is Curly. Homer can't look at Curly, who looks betrayed. Edna picks up Curly and carries him to the passenger-side window. Curly is sobbing.

HOMER

I have to go, Curly. I'm sorry.
(to Edna)
I couldn't find Buster. Will you tell him . . .

He can't finish what he has to say. Edna kisses him good-bye.

From the window, Larch watches the car leave.

Buster, whittling a stick, isn't watching.

INT./EXT. WALLY'S CAR—ON THE ROAD—AFTERNOON

There is quiet as the journey gets underway. Wally keeps glancing at Candy in the rear-view mirror; she seems distant, lost in thought. Homer is taking everything in—the speed, the road, the wind in his face.

INT. BOYS' DIVISION—NIGHT

Angela speaks to the boys.

ANGELA

Let us be happy for Homer Wells . . .

INT. GIRLS' DIVISION—NIGHT

In the girls' washroom, in front of the mirror by the row of sinks, Mary Agnes is repeatedly slapping her face. Angela's benediction to the boys plays Over this scene of violent self-abuse. Except for the sound of the slaps, Mary Agnes doesn't make a sound.

ANGELA (*O.S.*)

Homer Wells has found a family. Good night, Homer!

ALL THE BOYS (*O.S.*)

Good night, Homer!

INT. DISPENSARY—NIGHT

On his bed, Larch is taking ether. We hear the refrain from the boys in the bunk room Over.

ALL THE BOYS (*O.S.*)

Good night, Homer! Good night, Homer! Good night, Homer Wells!

INT. WALLY'S CAR—NIGHT

The radio is playing. Candy is lying down, her knees drawn up, in the backseat; she appears to be asleep, oblivious to Homer and Wally's conversation.

WALLY

Actually, the Army has given me leave twice. First when my father died, and now I'm on leave to help my mother—I'm just trying to get her ready for the harvest. She's no farmer. Apples were my dad's business. And with the war on, she's short on pickers.

Candy's eyes are open but her voice is groggy.

CANDY

(to Homer)
Wally thinks apples are boring.

WALLY

(to Homer)
I never said they were boring.

CANDY

You said, "Apples aren't exactly flying."

WALLY

Well, they aren't.

Homer looks back at Candy. Her eyes close.

HOMER

I think I'd probably like the apple business.

WALLY

You're a little overqualified, aren't you?

HOMER

No, I'm not. I need a job.

WALLY

The only jobs are picking jobs. Picking apples is truly boring.

Candy's eyes snap open and she sits up a little.

CANDY

There! You said it was boring.

WALLY

Well, *picking* them is! It's about as exciting as . . . walking!

Candy seems irritated with Wally. Homer tries to engage her.

HOMER

Is your family in the apple business, too?

CANDY

No, but I work there—I like it. My dad's a lobsterman.

HOMER

I've never seen a lobster.

CANDY

Really?

HOMER

I've never seen the ocean, either.

WALLY

(amazed)

You've never seen the *ocean*?

Homer shakes his head, smiles.

WALLY *(cont.)*

That's not funny . . . that's *serious*.

EXT./INT. ROADSIDE/CAR—NIGHT

The car is parked at the side of the road. Wally is half-hidden behind a tree. Candy and Homer are left alone in the car; there's an awkward silence as Homer pretends not to hear Wally's excessive peeing. Suddenly Candy starts to sob.

CANDY

I couldn't have a baby with someone who's leaving me—I didn't know what else to do!

Homer is a doctor—he's used to postabortion reactions.

HOMER

I know.

CANDY

He's going to be dropping bombs on Mandalay! They're going to be shooting at him!

HOMER

Where's Mandalay?

CANDY

Burma!

HOMER

Oh . . .

CANDY

I can't have a baby alone. I don't even know if he's coming back!

HOMER

I understand.

He doesn't, really. Wally returns. Wally leans over Candy to hug her.

WALLY

Honey, honey . . . of course I'll come back.

Candy pounds on his chest with her fists.

CANDY

You don't *know*, Wally. You have *no idea*!

Wally backs away. Candy sobs uncontrollably.

CANDY *(cont.)*

Stay away from me!

Wally signals to Homer to get out of the car.

Later, Wally and Homer stand outside the car, overhearing Candy's weeping. Homer is smoking nervously.

HOMER

(strictly medical)
This is all normal. Don't worry. The abortion procedure . . . it affects you. It's the ether, too. It'll take a little time.

WALLY

I don't *have* any time. There's a *war*!

HOMER

It's all very normal.

Wally looks at Homer, who takes a nervous drag on his cigarette.

WALLY

You ought to cut that shit out—it's terrible for you.

Homer looks at Wally; he sees the authority in his eyes. Homer drops his cigarette and puts it out with his foot.

They notice that Candy has stopped crying. Wally finds Candy asleep in the backseat.

EXT. WALLY'S CAR—ON THE ROAD—LATE AT NIGHT

The lone car on the road. Snatches of war news from the radio are the only sound as the headlights illuminate the dark highway.

EXT. COAST OF MAINE—MORNING

The car is parked, with Homer sleeping in it alone. The sounds from the ocean increase as Homer opens his eyes. Homer gets out of the car and walks toward the beach, enchanted. There it is: his first view ever of an ocean, the horizon, the sun glimmering on the water. Candy is lying on a blanket in the sand. Wally is throwing rocks in the water. Homer takes it all in. When Candy calls for him, Homer walks up to her.

CANDY

I'm a little worried about the . . .
(she gestures below her waist)
. . . about how much bleeding is okay.

HOMER

It should taper off tomorrow, but it can come back again. You have cramps?

(Candy nods)
They'll ease up, almost entirely. As long as the bleeding isn't heavy, it's normal.

WALLY *(O.S.)*

Catch!

A football comes flying though the air toward Homer; it bounces off his chest. Wally laughs.

WALLY *(cont.)*

(meaning the football)
Give it here!

Homer throws the football; it's clear he's never thrown one before.

WALLY *(cont.)*

What was *that*?! Come over here!

Homer runs over to Wally, who proceeds to show him how to pass the ball. Snatches of his instructions drift to Candy, who closes her eyes. "Put your fingers on the laces—no, it rests in your palm, like this! You want the laces up—yes, like that!"

EXT. COAST OF MAINE—DAY (LATER)

Homer and Wally sit on the beach a short distance from Candy's blanket. She appears to be asleep. Wally looks in her direction before he speaks to Homer.

WALLY

It's called the Burma run. It's about a seven-hour round-trip flight between India and China.

Wally draws a crude map in the sand.

HOMER

"Burma run" because you fly over Burma . . .

WALLY

And over the Himalayas. That's called flying over the hump.

On Candy's face: she's not asleep, she's listening.

HOMER (*O.S.*)

At what altitude?

WALLY (*O.S.*)

I've got thirty-five minutes to climb to fifteen thousand feet—that's the first mountain pass.

Homer looks at Wally, thoughtfully.

HOMER

What lousy luck—I mean your orders . . . to draw an assignment like that!

WALLY

(conspiratorially)
Actually, I volunteered.

Homer is shocked; he looks back at Candy, lowers his voice.

HOMER

It's the flying, right? You love to fly, don't you?

Wally nods; he also gives a look in Candy's direction before he responds.

WALLY

I love the bombing, too. But there's also the Himalayas—they have the most wicked air currents in the world. I wouldn't miss flying there for anything.

Homer's smile suggests that he's impressed, but that he wouldn't have Wally's enthusiasm for the task. Wally laughs and puts his hand on Homer's shoulder.

WALLY *(cont.)*

Uh, look . . . if you're serious about wanting a job, picking apples isn't that boring.

HOMER

Oh, I would love that, Wally.

EXT. CAPE KENNETH—LOBSTER POUND—AFTERNOON

The car is parked at a lobster pound. Homer sits in the car watching Wally carrying Candy's bag to the door. Candy stands outside the car; she shakes Homer's hand.

CANDY

I guess I'll see you around the orchards. Thanks for everything.

HOMER

Sure . . . I'll see you around.

Candy turns and heads toward the house to catch up with Wally. A lobsterman in his boat is approaching the dock. It's RAY, *Candy's father. Candy waves.* "Hi, Daddy!" *Homer glances at Candy and Wally on the dock, kissing goodbye.*

CANDY

(whispering)

I love you, Wally.

WALLY

I love you, too. See you tomorrow.

EXT. OCEAN VIEW—WORTHINGTON HOUSE—LATE AFTERNOON

Wally drives up to the Worthington house; he gets out of the car. Homer sits in the car, admiring the beautiful farmhouse.

WALLY

Come on. You have to meet my mom.
(conspiratorially)
If it comes up, I've been at a wedding. That's where I met you, at the wedding.

INT. WORTHINGTON HOUSE—WALLY'S BEDROOM—LATE AFTERNOON

Homer has never seen such a room: the sports trophies, the photos of athletic teams, and of Candy with Wally. Model airplanes are everywhere. Mrs. Worthington's voice comes from the hall.

OLIVE (*O.S.*)

Wally? I expected you earlier . . .

She appears in the doorway of Wally's room. Mrs. Worthington (OLIVE) *is an elegant, fiftyish New Englander, as handsome as Wally, but more reserved. She is surprised to see Homer.*

WALLY

This is Homer Wells, Mom—he's the most overqualified apple picker you'll ever meet, but he's dying to learn the apple business.

Wally is taking his uniform off as he speaks, just dropping it on the floor as he quickly puts on some farm clothes.

OLIVE

How do you do, Homer Wells . . .

Homer has never met anyone like her.

HOMER

How do you do . . .

Mrs. Worthington starts picking up her son's uniform from the floor. She is politely curious about Homer.

OLIVE

Were you a friend of the bride or the groom?

Homer looks confused; he seems to have forgotten about the alleged wedding. Wally puts his arm around Homer, urging him into the hall.

WALLY

Homer is everybody's friend, Mom . . . the bride's, the groom's, mine, Candy's, *everybody's.*

Homer is embarrassed, but Olive is obdurately well-mannered.

OLIVE

Well, perhaps you'll come to dinner, Homer . . .

Wally calls to her as he pushes Homer down the hall,

WALLY

Not tonight, Mom—he's got to meet *Mr. Rose!*

EXT. CIDER HOUSE—DUSK

Homer and Wally get out of the Jeep at the cider house, a barnlike building with adjacent sheds and, behind it, line after line of trees—the apple orchards.

Homer sees an outdoor shower where THREE BLACK MEN *are showering. It is a wooden stall that leaves the shower's occupants visible above and below their midsections.* A FOURTH BLACK MAN *is caught naked, running behind the cider house and out of sight as he wraps a towel around himself.*

JACK

You already used up the hot water!

MUDDY

You're usin' my soap, ain't you?

JACK

I ain't usin' no soap—it's too cold to bother with soap!

MUDDY

There ain't never enough hot water, soap or no soap.

WALLY

They're migrants.

HOMER

(no clue)
Migrants?

WALLY

Yes. They pick fruit, all kinds. They travel up and down the coast with the seasons.
(leaning close to Homer)
The trick to Mr. Rose is, you have to let him be the boss.

Homer wonders what that means as Wally reaches for the door of the cider house. Before Wally can knock, a pretty young black girl, ROSE ROSE, *bumps open the screen door with her hip and throws a bucket of water in the grass—almost hitting Homer and Wally.*

ROSE ROSE

That sink's backed up again, Wally. I thought you was gonna get me a plumber.

WALLY

Rose, this is Homer—Homer, this is Mr. Rose's daughter, Rose.

HOMER

Rose Rose?

ROSE ROSE

Pretty, ain't it? You a plumber?

WALLY

No, no—Homer is a new *picker*. He's going to stay here with you.

This gets the attention of the men on their way from the showers. They walk over, towels around their waists.

ROSE ROSE

(suspiciously)

He's stayin' *here*?

The screen door swings open and shut again, startling them all, as MR. ROSE *comes out of the cider house.*

MR. ROSE

That daughter of mine sure is Miss Hospitality, ain't she, Wally?

Grinning, Mr. Rose shakes Wally's hand. Rose Rose goes back inside the cider house as Mr. Rose shakes Homer's hand. Homer introduces himself.

MR. ROSE *(cont.)*

You got lots of experience pickin', I suppose.

WALLY

Homer's got no experience, Arthur, but he's smarter than I am. He's a fast learner.

Mr. Rose looks briefly at the men, who wait for his reaction.

MR. ROSE

This is history. Ain't that what you're sayin', Wally? I guess we makin' *history* . . . havin' this young man stay with us!

Wally slaps Homer on the back; he goes inside the cider house to help Rose Rose with the plumbing.

WALLY

(over his shoulder)
See you later.

Homer looks at Mr. Rose for instructions. Mr. Rose stares back at him with his enigmatic smile.

HOMER

So. What should I do now?

MR. ROSE

Out back, there's a shed. It's just a mess. If that shed was better organized, I could put my truck in there.

Homer looks at Mr. Rose with an uncomprehending expression.

MR. ROSE *(cont.)*

If you're as smart as Wally says, you know you sometimes gotta do one job before you do another.

Homer thinks that over.

Later, Homer is cleaning out the shed.

EXT. CIDER HOUSE—EVENING

The pickers all sit down to supper around a picnic table. Homer with Mr. Rose, Rose Rose, and the other black pickers. Mr. Rose takes an apple from a bowl on the table. Then he pulls out a knife and opens it in one fluid motion; he's so fast, the knife seems to come out of nowhere. He begins to peel the apple. Homer eyes Mr. Rose, but Mr. Rose's focus is riveted to his apple and the long, perfect strand of peel dangling from it.

MR. ROSE

You did a good job with that shed, Homer.

Peaches breaks the awkward silence.

PEACHES

What kind of name is Homer?

HOMER

It's the name of a cat. Originally. Well, not *originally*.

Homer decides to stop. Another silence.

MR. ROSE

Now, now—we all got names, sensible or not.
(to Homer)
Peaches is from Georgia, where we met him pickin' peaches. He's still better with peaches than he is with apples.
(Peaches grins)
Jack here is new. And this here is Hero, 'cause he was a hero of some kind or other once. Ain't that right, Hero?

(There are some disrespectful suggestions from the pickers concerning what his heroism might have been.)

MR. ROSE *(cont.)*

And this here sensitive-lookin' fella is Muddy. The less said about Muddy, the better. Ain't that right, Muddy?

Muddy scowls at Homer, but he smiles at Mr. Rose.

INT. BUNKHOUSE—NIGHT

Homer unpacks his suitcase. (His bed should be nearest Muddy's and Mr. Rose's.) Jack lies on his bed, smoking. Muddy, also smoking, is sitting on his bed, sharpening a knife. Hero and Peaches are playing cards on one of their beds. Mr. Rose is finishing shaving. Rose Rose watches Homer unpack.

ROSE ROSE

What's that?

HOMER

It's just my heart.

ROSE ROSE

What you got a picture of your heart for?

He holds up the X ray, in order to show her.

HOMER

There's a little something wrong with it. Just this part here—the right ventricle. It's slightly enlarged.

ROSE ROSE

So what?

HOMER

Yes, so what. It's nothing serious, really. Just a small defect.

MR. ROSE

It's big enough to keep you out of the war, I suppose. Ain't that right?

HOMER

Right.

Rose Rose picks up the book that Homer has put on the bed. She studies the cover; it's Great Expectations *by Charles Dickens. She puts it down, restlessly.*

MR. ROSE

They told me I was too old to serve.

PEACHES

They told Muddy his feet was too flat!

Everybody laughs, except Muddy.

MUDDY

(to Peaches)
And you was "generally unfit," as I recall.

Finished unpacking, Homer sits on his bed; he picks up Great Expectations *and begins to read. Rose Rose sits down next to him, watching him read. Homer notices her interest.*

HOMER

Do you like to read?

ROSE ROSE

(embarrassed)
I can't read. Nobody taught me.

Homer smiles politely and goes back to his book. Rose Rose keeps looking over his shoulder at the pages.

ROSE ROSE *(cont.)*

(pointing to the page)
What does it say there?

Homer looks around at the pickers lying in their beds, smoking, listening. (Like bedtime stories at the orphanage, he thinks; however, the pickers' attitude is suspicious, reserved.)

HOMER

(reading)
"I looked at the stars, and considered how awful it would be for a man to turn his face to them as he froze to death, and see no help or pity in all the glittering multitude."

Homer looks up; there's no response.

HOMER *(cont.)*

(to Rose Rose)
More?

Some muttering, some giggling, mostly silence. Rose Rose wants more, but suddenly Jack jumps out of bed and stomps to the kitchen end of the cider house, where a piece of paper is tacked to the wall. Jack is talking to Homer all the way.

JACK

Since you're the one who's smart enough to read . . . what's this?

Jack points at the piece of paper. Homer gets up and looks at it.

HOMER

It's a list of rules, it seems.

All the men groan—Jack swears and Peaches laughs.

ROSE ROSE

Whose rules?

MUDDY

They're for us, I suppose.

JACK

Go on and read 'em, Homer.

HOMER

"One. Please don't smoke in bed."

ROSE ROSE

It's too late for that one!

All the smokers laugh and cough in their beds.

MR. ROSE

(uncharacteristically blunt)

Stop it, Homer. They aren't our rules. We didn't write them. I don't see no reason to read them.

HOMER

Okay . . .

Rose Rose stomps back to her bed. Her father absently snaps his towel.

INT. BUNKHOUSE—NIGHT (LATER)

Everybody is asleep, except Homer. He is staring at the ceiling in the quiet semi-darkness, the book lying on his chest.

LARCH (*O.S.*)

(distant, echoing)

Good night, you Princes of Maine! You Kings of New England!

INT. BOYS' DIVISION—NIGHT

Dr. Larch is standing in the doorway to the boys' room; he closes the door.

INT. BUNKHOUSE—NIGHT

Homer, on his bed, closes his eyes.

INT. DISPENSARY—NIGHT

Larch lies in bed with his eyes open. (No ether.)

EXT. CIDER HOUSE—NIGHT

The cider house and the apple orchard in the moonlight.

EXT. ORCHARDS—MORNING

Wally in his farm clothes at the wheel of the Jeep—he is racing through the orchards, dodging trees, with Homer in the passenger seat, hanging on for dear life.

WALLY

Remember this! In the morning, when the tall grass is wet, you can make the Jeep slide on the grass. Can you feel it?

Homer is excited as Wally weaves among the trees—faster and faster.

WALLY *(cont.)*

It's almost like flying.

HOMER

What about the trees?

WALLY

The trees are flak—antiaircraft fire from those geeks on the ground.

Wally brakes hard. The Jeep comes to a stop in the packing-house area.

Candy has been waiting on the loading platform. The pickers are working in the background.

WALLY *(cont.)*

(defensively to Candy)
I was just showing Homer the orchards . . . kind of a geography lesson.

CANDY

(good-naturedly)
I know what you've been doing.

She pulls an apple branch, with an apple or two, out of the vehicle's grille—or else the branch is wedged in the front-bumper or headlight area. Candy playfully starts poking Wally with the branch.

CANDY *(cont.)*

(to Wally)
You've been giving him a *flying* lesson!

WALLY

(teasing her)
He *loved* it!
(to Homer)
Didn't you?

HOMER

Yeah, it was great.

Wally gets the apple branch away from Candy. He pins her arms at her sides—he hugs her, kisses her. She doesn't struggle.

CANDY

(laughing to Homer)
He thinks people *like* to get whacked by branches.

WALLY

Homer liked it!
(to Homer)
Didn't you?

HOMER

Yeah, sure. There's no stress or strain around here . . .

They all laugh. Homer observes the happy couple.

EXT. ORCHARDS—DAY

Homer is walking with Wally and Candy. The orchards are beautiful.

EXT. PACKING HOUSE—MORNING

Much activity: the pickers are unloading apple crates from a full flatbed trailer. An angry-looking VERNON *gives Homer an evil glare. Homer spills some apples lifting the crate to the loading platform.*

VERNON

What's wrong with you?

Mr. Rose takes Homer aside.

MR. ROSE

That's Vernon. You best stay away from him until he gets to know you better—then you best stay away from him *more!*

Wally, in full uniform, appears from inside the packing house; he calls for Homer.

MR. ROSE *(cont.)*

Our lieutenant's calling you, Homer. Mind your ass.

Homer smiles and runs toward Wally.

INT./EXT. PACKING HOUSE—MORNING

Homer and Wally walk through the packing house, where the HEFTY, LOUD WOMEN *sort through the apples rolling by on the conveyor tracks. Wally snatches an apple from one of them, giving it to Homer.*

WALLY

(to Homer)

You getting along okay?

Before Homer can answer, the women interrupt.

BIG DOT

Where is that Candy?

FLORENCE

Did she leave you, Wally?

DEBRA

Who's the boy?

Wally makes an effort to introduce Homer, but he's interrupted.

FLORENCE

Wally, you can marry Debra if Candy leaves you!

BIG DOT

Wally's gonna marry *me* if Candy leaves him!

DEBRA

You can marry all three of us, Wally!

FLORENCE

We can take turns.

Wally puts his hand to his heart.

WALLY

You girls make it hard for a guy to go off to war.
(points to Homer)
But I'll leave my best man here to pinch-hit for me.

As the women are left behind giggling, Wally continues talking to Homer.

WALLY *(cont.)*

Uh . . . I'm shipping out sooner than I thought. I just wanted to be sure you were settled in—and happy enough, considering . . .
(grabbing another apple from a crate)
Are you bored stiff? Or can you stick it out for a bit?

HOMER

Uh . . . actually, picking apples is as much excitement as I want for a while. I'm grateful for the job.

WALLY

(his hand on Homer's shoulder)
You're the one who's helping *me*, Homer. You're going to give my mom a little peace of mind while I'm gone. Candy, too.

HOMER

Well, sure . . . that's good, then.
(awkward pause)
All I mean is, I'm lucky I met you.

WALLY

I don't think so, Homer. *I'm* the lucky one.

Homer shakes his head. Wally stops walking; they both stop.

WALLY *(cont.)*

(more serious)
You want to fight about it?

Homer is unfamiliar with this kind of kidding around; at first he is startled, but then he laughs. Wally laughs, too. They shake hands.

Mr. Rose calls out to Homer from the tractor. The pickers are impatiently waiting for him on the flatbed; they're going back to the orchard. Homer has to run to catch up to them. He jumps on the flatbed; he sees Wally waving good-bye.

EXT. ORCHARDS—DAY

High up in a tall tree on a couple of ladders, Mr. Rose and Homer are picking side by side. Mr. Rose is picking with high-speed perfection, but Homer is slower and fumbling—he drops an occasional apple to the ground.

MR. ROSE

You pickin' more cider apples than anythin' else. Them drops is good only for cider. And you pickin' the stems with the apples only half the time. They good only for cider, too—if you don't pick them stems.
(Homer watches him)
The rule is, you wanna pick the apple *with* the stem, Homer. And see here . . . see that *bud* that's just above the stem? That's the bud for *next year's* apple—that's called the *spur*. You pick the spur, you pickin' two years in one—you pickin' next year's apple 'fore it have a chance to grow. You leave that on the branch, you hear?

Homer nods; he picks more carefully, with more concentration.

MR. ROSE *(cont.)*

(approvingly)
That's better. I can tell you got yourself some education. Them's good hands you got, Homer. Them hands you got, they know what they're doin'—ain't that right?

HOMER

I guess so . . .

Homer can see over the apple mart parking lot from the top of the tree. He can see the driveway of the Worthington house, where Candy and Olive are saying a tearful good-bye to Wally. Distracted, Homer drops another couple of apples, which Mr. Rose observes with a wry smile.

ANGELA (*O.S.*)

Wilbur! Wilbur!

INT. LARCH'S OFFICE—DAY

Larch is doing something at his desk when Angela comes in.

ANGELA

Wilbur, you should read this.

Larch stares at Angela, who holds a letter.

ANGELA *(cont.)*

It's from the Board. Another letter.

INT. LARCH'S OFFICE—NIGHT

Dr. Larch stands in front of a mechanical drawing easel. He works intently with a calligraphic pen, but we don't see what he's working on. Angela and Edna sit at the desk; they're looking over the letter.

ANGELA

(quoting the letter)

Uh . . . "merely suggesting that some new blood might benefit you all . . . someone with new ideas in the obstetrical and pediatric fields."

(she looks up at Larch)

I think they're just testing some ideas for our next meeting.

EDNA

Dr. Holtz seems nice. I think he only wants to help . . .

LARCH

He is a goddamn psychiatrist—of *course* he wants to "help"! He'd be happy if he could help *commit* me!

ANGELA

It's that Mrs. Goodhall you have to be careful of, Wilbur.

LARCH

One has to be more than "careful" of Mrs. Goodhall—she has sufficient Christian zeal to start her own country! I'd like to give her a little ether.

EDNA

So what are you going to do?

Larch puts down the pen, comes around the easel, opens a drawer in a filing cabinet, and hands Edna a folder containing a few cleanly typed pages. Larch returns to the easel, to his painstaking work. Edna opens the file; as she and Angela read the contents, Larch recites from memory as he works.

LARCH

"Homer Wells, born Portland, Maine, March 2, 1915 . . ."

EDNA

Homer was born *here*, in, what was it, 1922?

LARCH

". . . graduated Bowdoin College, 1935, and Harvard School of Medicine, 1939."

ANGELA

This is *your* life story, Wilbur! You just changed the dates!

LARCH

"An internship and two years of training at the Boston Lying-in, South End Branch. For his age, he was judged an accomplished gynecological and obstetrical surgeon; he is also experienced in pediatric care . . ."

ANGELA

You *invented* him! You've completely made him up!

LARCH

Don't you understand? The Board is going to *replace* me! That's what the "new blood" is *for*!

EDNA

You mean they'll replace you with someone who won't perform abortions.

LARCH

(sarcastically)

Well, we can only guess about that, Edna. They *are* against the law.

ANGELA

These *credentials* are against the law!

LARCH

We all know who trained Homer—his credentials are as good as mine are. Don't you be holy to me about the *law*! What has the law done for any of us here?

Edna and Angela think this over.

LARCH *(cont.)*

(points at file)

So here is my candidate. What do you think?

EDNA

But what about school records? Homer doesn't have any *diplomas . . .*

Larch turns the easel around. Attached is a parchment headed: "HARVARD MEDICAL SCHOOL"—*it's a diploma-in-progress.*

LARCH

He *will* have them, Edna.

The women are shocked, awed.

ANGELA

Oh, Wilbur, I don't know . . .

(sudden thought)

We don't even know where he is!

EXT. CIDER HOUSE, ROOF—NIGHT

ROSE ROSE *(O.S.)*

Where's that Homer?

Homer stands in front of a ladder that leans against the cider house; he starts to climb up, drawn by the murmuring voices, the soft laughter.

JACK *(O.S.)*

Who cares?

MR. ROSE *(O.S.)*

Now, now. He's a good boy.

JACK *(O.S.)*

Shit. We don't know what he is.

MR. ROSE *(O.S.)*

Jack, you gotta watch your language 'round my daughter.

Homer arrives at the top and sees everyone sitting on a long plank, a bench attached to the apex of the roof—obviously a popular spot.

MR. ROSE *(cont.)*

Here he is.

No one moves.

MR. ROSE *(cont.)*

Where's your manners? Make room for Homer, so's he can enjoy the view.

MUDDY

What view?

Peaches slides over and Homer sits down.

HOMER

Are we supposed to be up here? The rules said . . .

MR. ROSE

Homer, you the only one who's read them rules, so you the only one who feels like he's doin' somethin' wrong.

The others laugh.

MUDDY

What view?

MR. ROSE

Well, Muddy, we can look at all these angry stars Homer's been readin' to us about.

More laughter; Homer smiles, enjoying the teasing.

JACK

(gesturing toward the Worthington farmhouse)
I bet the view looks better from the Worthin'tons'.

MR. ROSE

You think so, Jack? Well . . . I wouldn't want to be in that Wally's shoes tonight.

ROSE ROSE

(playfully, teasing him)
Daddy, I'd like to be in that Wally's shoes *every* night.

MR. ROSE

(teasing her back)
You lucky you in your work boots tonight, girl . . .

ROSE ROSE

What's lucky about that?

Rose Rose is being physically affectionate with her father—lightly punching his arm, rubbing the top of his head.

MR. ROSE

You know where that Wally is tonight, darlin'? He's up there in them angry stars.
(gesturing at the dark sky)
He's flyin' all around up there . . . with them Japs shooting at him.

They all look up, imagining that. Homer more than the others. Rose Rose, looking thoughtful, rests her head on her father's shoulder. They are completely natural together.

EXT. CAPE KENNETH—APPLE MART—DAY

Homer and the pickers are loading crates of apples into a shipping truck. Olive and Candy are consulting some papers (the shipping tally) on a clipboard; Mr. Rose is standing beside them.

MR. ROSE

They all on board, Mrs. Worthin'ton.

OLIVE

Thank you, Arthur.
(she is looking at Homer)
And how is our Homer working out?

She catches Homer's eye; he smiles, then joins them. Mr. Rose puts his arm around him.

MR. ROSE

Oh, he's a smart young man, most of the time—Wally was right about him.

Olive is looking over the rest of the picking crew.

OLIVE

No rotten apples?

MR. ROSE

(it's an old way of speaking that they have)

No, no—not this year. Well . . . maybe we got *one*, but it ain't Homer.

He means Jack, who gives Olive and Candy and Mr. Rose a furtive look. Olive smiles at Rose Rose, who comes up to her and Candy. Olive touches Rose Rose with affection.

OLIVE

Rose . . . dear girl, I'm sure I can find you some other clothes.

(to Candy)

You must have some things that would fit her.

Candy takes Rose Rose by the shoulders and turns her around. Rose Rose is enjoying this.

CANDY

I have a *ton* of things that would fit you.

MR. ROSE

Now, now, Candy—this girl don't need no more clothes, not for pickin'.

He starts leading his daughter away.

OLIVE

(charming)

Arthur, there's no such thing as a young woman who's got all the clothes she needs.

Olive waves good-bye as she moves toward her car. Candy turns to Homer.

CANDY

So. Not bored yet?

HOMER

I'm *never* bored! It's all very . . . different for me . . . here.

Homer has the hardest time looking at Candy.

HOMER *(cont.)*

Uh . . . have you been *feeling* okay?

CANDY

When I'm not thinking about Wally. I'm not good at being alone.

(realizing)

Oh, goodness. You meant . . . yes, I'm fine. I . . .

(struggling to change the subject)

. . . I don't suppose you've seen a lobster yet.

Homer shakes his head. He looks at the tractor and the empty trailer. Mr. Rose and the pickers are just watching them.

CANDY *(cont.)*

(more seriously)

You have to come to my dad's lobster pound and see one, then.

HOMER

Okay . . .

Homer looks toward the pickers sitting on the flatbed when he hears the tractor start. Candy follows his gaze.

HOMER *(cont.)*

I better go.

CANDY

I don't think Mr. Rose would leave without you.

Mr. Rose gestures for Muddy to drive off; the tractor trailer pulls away.

CANDY *(cont.)*

(laughing)

Sorry!

Homer has to run to catch up.

CANDY *(cont.)*

(calling)
Come next week!

He jumps on the back of the departing flatbed between Mr. Rose and Rose Rose, as Candy watches him.

INT. BUNKHOUSE—DUSK

An anxious-looking WHITE PLUMBER *is fixing the kitchen sink while the pickers (in their towels) stand around and watch.*

Homer is putting on his best shirt. Peaches admires the shirt as Rose Rose cooks the night's supper on the wood stove.

PEACHES

Whoa—look at that Homer! He's gettin' all dressed up for supper tonight!

ROSE ROSE

He ain't gettin' dressed to have supper with *us*, Peaches!

The pickers all look at Homer, who looks guilty as he leaves.

MR. ROSE

(to the plumber)
Don't let us make you nervous or nothin'—we know you gotta job to do.

MUDDY

Yeah, we can wait all night for the water to come back on—you just go on and take your time.

EXT. INLAND ROAD—DUSK

Homer pedals a bicycle down a dirt road.

EXT. LOBSTER POUND—DUSK

Ray holds a lobster up to the camera. We see the old-fashioned wooden pens, floating dockside.

RAY

Hungry?

Homer looks uncertain.

EXT. GANGPLANK, DOCK—DUSK

Homer and Ray and Candy go up the gangplank from the dock to the lobster pound.

RAY

They're the garbage-eaters of the ocean's floor. The seagulls clean up the shore. The lobsters clean up the bottom of the sea.

HOMER

They eat everything?

RAY

Everything that falls to the bottom.

CANDY

It's time somebody ate *them*.

RAY

(*to Candy*)
I was lookin' for Wally's letter. I was gonna show it to Homer . . .

(to Homer)
They made him a captain already—*Captain* Worthington!

CANDY

Daddy, it's a letter to *me*.

RAY

He mentions Homer, too, you know.

CANDY

(awkwardly)
Wally said to say, "Hello."

HOMER

(equally awkward)
Oh! That's . . . nice.

RAY

(to Homer)
Wally said the most spectacular hits were in the oil fields at Yenangyat.

Later, through the window of the lobster pound, we see them eating lobster around a kitchen table. Laughter and some unclear dialogue drift to us.

EXT./INT. CAPE KENNETH/WALLY'S CAR—NIGHT

With the bicycle stowed in the trunk, Candy is driving Homer back to the cider house. They pass a drive-in movie theater, the marquee announcing "CLOSED FOR THE SEASON." Homer stares in awe at the giant blank screen.

HOMER

A movie *outside?*

CANDY

Yes. But it's closed all the time now, because of the blackout.

HOMER

People watched the movies in their cars?

CANDY

(smiling)
When they watched at all. Do you like movies?

HOMER

Yes! I've seen only one, though.

Candy looks at him; he isn't joking.

CANDY

You've seen only one movie? Which one?

HOMER

King Kong. It's really good.

Candy laughs.

CANDY

I haven't seen *King Kong* since I was a kid!

Homer laughs a little self-consciously; around her, he feels like he's still *a kid.*

INT. DINING HALL—EARLY MORNING

At one table, the children are happily eating apples; a few of the kids are stuffing apples from a big bowl into their pockets. At another table, Larch, Edna, and Angela sit around an open packing crate of apples. Larch takes a bite from an apple and spits it out. Angela takes the apple out of his hand.

ANGELA

That's a pie apple, Wilbur. Homer said you're not supposed to eat it!

Angela hands him another apple.

LARCH

So he's an apple expert, is he?

Angela gives him a critical look as Larch takes a bite out of the new apple.

LARCH *(cont.)*

(sarcastically)

Oh my, yes! This is a *far* superior taste—and crisp, too! You know, so many apples are disappointingly mealy. I wonder if most of the apples in my life weren't meant for pies!

ANGELA

Wilbur, he picked them for us himself . . .

LARCH

(incredulous)

You don't find it depressing that Homer Wells is picking apples?

Both Edna and Angela glower at him.

LARCH *(cont.)*

Or that he can't be bothered to write us a proper letter? A dissertation on apples, we don't need!

EDNA

(annoyed)

He probably doesn't make much money picking apples—he must have had to pay to send them, too.

LARCH

I wouldn't worry, Edna, that he doesn't have money. If he gets hungry, he can pick his dinner!

Larch angrily tosses the half-eaten apple into the garbage.

EDNA

Wilbur, it's a *gift*! How can you be angry with Homer for sending us a *gift*?

Larch stares into space, depressed. Then he examines the crate and finds the mailing label that says "OCEAN VIEW ORCHARDS—CAPE KENNETH, MAINE." *He rips it off, holds it up triumphantly.*

LARCH

I'll show him a *gift*! I'll give him a gift he can *use*!

Larch storms out of the room.

INT. CAPE KENNETH—MOVIE THEATER—NIGHT

A newsreel from the war is playing on the screen—soldiers marching, smiling, waving to the camera. Homer and Candy sit together watching. Homer is completely fascinated; Candy watches Homer as much as the news. Her expression changes when the newsreel cuts to footage from an air raid.

EXT. CAPE KENNETH—MOVIE THEATER—NIGHT

Candy and Homer walk out of the theater, under the marquee and past the poster for Wuthering Heights.

CANDY

(disappointed)
But you looked as if you liked it.

HOMER

(smiling)
I *did* like it. All I said was, "It's no *King Kong*."

Candy makes a face, but in good fun.

HOMER *(cont.)*

First she loved him, then she didn't, then no one else could have him . . .

CANDY

She *did* love him!
(teasing him)
How many women have you known?

Homer is embarrassed; he ducks the question.

HOMER

And what did she die of, exactly?

CANDY

She was torn apart! She died of a broken heart.

HOMER

Oh, sure!

Homer smiles and shakes his head; Candy starts to laugh.

HOMER *(cont.)*

What's the *medical* explanation?

CANDY

Well, she was in a weakened condition . . .
(laughs)
I don't know! What about King Kong?! Is that medically possible?

Homer smiles; he knows she's teasing him, and he likes it.

HOMER

(mock serious)
At least King Kong knew what he *wanted*.

Candy pushes him playfully. They're both having a good time, too *good a time.*

EXT. ORCHARDS—DAY

Homer is picking apples in a big tree; Rose Rose is on a ladder in the tree right beside him. She's picking about twice as fast as he is, and he keeps dropping his apples. In another tree, Muddy is watching.

ROSE ROSE

What is you *doin'* with that Candy, Homer?

MUDDY

(*imitating Mr. Rose*)

He's makin' history, I suppose.

From the surrounding trees, the other pickers laugh.

ROSE ROSE

You ain't gettin' in no trouble, I hope.

HOMER

No trouble.

In adjacent trees, both Peaches and Hero are picking apples; they can hear Homer and Rose Rose, too. (So can Mr. Rose.)

PEACHES

That Candy—she's the nicest girl I know!

MUDDY

She's about the most beautiful girl I ever seen—I don't know if she's the nicest.

HOMER

She's the nicest *and* the most beautiful girl I've ever known.

The men oooh *and* aaah *at Homer's announcement—Mr. Rose, too.*

ROSE ROSE

That sounds like you is in trouble already, Homer.

MR. ROSE

That's right—that sounds like trouble to me.

HOMER

I'm not in trouble.

ROSE ROSE

Yeah, you is. I know when people is in trouble, and you is.

Camera closes on Homer's face; he keeps picking.

LARCH (*O.S.*)

His name is Homer Wells . . .

INT. ST. CLOUD'S—DINING HALL—EVENING

Edna and Angela face the Board of Trustees around a table. Larch circles the table as everyone reads the contents of a folder. Larch has provided a copy for each member. The three elderly gentlemen on the Board don't speak; they just nod their heads to everything Dr. Holtz or Mrs. Goodhall says.

LARCH

. . . and his *pathetic* resume is the best I've seen. Though I find it hard to believe the Board would be interested in this character.

DR. HOLTZ

But he looks like an excellent young man, a first-rate candidate!

LARCH

He looks like a bleeding-heart missionary *moron* to me, but that's going to be the problem with any doctor interested in coming here!

MRS. GOODHALL

Do you know him?

LARCH

No! I don't want to know him! He's doing *missionary* work—in *India!* I wrote him *weeks* ago, but he's either too holy or too busy to answer. Maybe he got killed in the war!

Suddenly Steerforth bursts through the door, having been pushed from behind by Mary Agnes. The two stop when they see what's going on—not to mention Larch's stern expression. They back out, Mary Agnes winking at Dr. Holtz before the door closes. Mrs. Goodhall is ready to continue.

MRS. GOODHALL

I fail to see how someone courageous enough to make a commitment to a foreign mission is automatically to be dismissed—that part of the world requires precisely the kind of dedication that is needed here.

LARCH

Does it *snow* in Bombay? One winter here and we'll be shipping him south, in a *coffin!*

MRS. GOODHALL

You can't think that a man who has *served* under such conditions as exist over there will be in the slightest daunted by a little *snow*—have you no idea how harsh and primitive and full of *disease* that part of the world is?

LARCH

Then I suppose we can look forward to catching various diseases from him!

DR. HOLTZ

But, Dr. Larch, he seems exceptionally qualified . . .

LARCH

I'm not talking about his medical qualifications. It's the *Christian* thing that bothers me—I just don't see it being of much *use* around here.

MRS. GOODHALL

(*bitterly*)
I fail to see how a little Christianity could *hurt* anyone here!

LARCH

Anyway, I was just showing you this guy as an example of what's available—I didn't think you'd be interested.

DR. HOLTZ

We're *very* interested!

MRS. GOODHALL

Yes, *very*!

DR. HOLTZ

You wouldn't be opposed to meeting with him?

LARCH

I suppose it wouldn't hurt to *meet* him. What's his name again?

ANGELA

Dr. Homer Wells.

LARCH

(*mumbling*)

I just hope he won't expect us to say *Grace* all the time.

The three elderly gentlemen repeat the name.

MRS. GOODHALL

It's a nice name, very New England.

DR. HOLTZ

Very *Maine*, a very *local*-sounding name.

EDNA

Very!

INT. DISPENSARY—NIGHT

A song plays on the old phonograph as a happy Larch and Angela dance. Edna interrupts them.

EDNA

I just wanted to ask you . . .

LARCH

Edna! Come dance with me! Let's be foolish tonight.

EDNA

Does he *know* he's supposed to be in India? Does he even *want* to come back?

This causes Larch to take the needle off the record.

LARCH

(*angrily*)

He's a field hand! What could possibly hold him there?

EXT. CIDER HOUSE—RAINY DAY

The rain beats down on Olive's car. Homer gets soaking wet as he leans in to talk to Candy, who's behind the wheel. Mr. Rose calls to Homer from the doorway of the mill room.

INT. MILL ROOM—RAINY DAY

Mr. Rose is instructing Homer as they stand bottling cider in their yellow slickers and rubber boots. Rose Rose is hosing down the pressboards; Muddy and Hero and Peaches are operating the grinder and the press. Jack is stirring the vat. In a defiant, contemptuous way, Jack keeps flicking the ash of his cigarette into the vat. This makes everyone uncomfortable; only Mr. Rose doesn't appear to notice.

MR. ROSE

Cider don't have no taste till later in October—it's too watery now, when we're usin' just them early Macs and them Gravensteins. You don't get no *good* cider till you're pickin' them Golden Delicious and them Winter Bananas, them Baldwins and them Russets . . .

HOMER

What about the worms? Most of these apples are the drops—off the ground, right? There have to be worms.

MR. ROSE

Of *course* there's worms, Homer! And what is them worms, really? They just *protein*, them worms! They is *good* for you!

Everyone but Jack laughs. He takes a last drag on his cigarette, then deliberately drops it into the vat.

MR. ROSE *(cont.)*

That just ain't right, Jack—your cigarette's gonna end up in nine or ten gallons of this batch of cider! That ain't right.

JACK

Them people drinkin' that cider, they don't know there's a cigarette in there!

MR. ROSE

It's not that hard to find it in there, Jack—it'll take you just a minute. You just gotta go fishin'.

JACK

You mean *swimmin'*. I ain't goin' in that vat to fish out no cigarette!

MR. ROSE

What business is you in, Jack? Just tell me what your business is . . .

Jack looks for a translation from the other men, who are nervous.

MUDDY

Just say you're in the *apple* business, man. That's the only business you wanna be in. Just say it.

Jack pulls a knife on Mr. Rose.

PEACHES

(*whispers excitedly to Jack*)
You don't wanna go in the knife business with Mistuh Rose—just say you're in the *apple* business, Jack!

JACK

(*to Mr. Rose*)
What business are *you* in?

We never see Mr. Rose's knife. We see the men circle each other: Jack takes a swipe at Mr. Rose's head—then he steps back, his yellow slicker slashed open. His slicker is opened up, right up the middle. His shirt underneath the slicker is slashed open, too—he feels his bare chest and stomach, feeling for the cut. But there's no cut—Jack's not bleeding, he's not even scratched. Just his clothes have been slashed.

MR. ROSE

I'm in the *knife* business, Jack. You don't wanna go in the knife business with me.

Muddy turns Jack around and views his slashed clothes.

MUDDY

You're lucky he didn't cut your *nipples* off, man.

PEACHES

The good news, Jack, is you're half-undressed for *swimmin'* . . .

MUDDY

Yeah, that cigarette ain't hard to find when you're properly undressed.

Jack starts to undress for the vat.

Mr. Rose ushers Homer and Rose Rose outside.

INT. BUNKHOUSE—RAINY DAY

Mr. Rose has cut his own hand in the fight. Homer's professionalism is offended to watch Rose Rose's amateurish efforts to stitch up her father's wound, but clearly this isn't the first time she's done it.

HOMER

Give me that. I know how to do it.

ROSE ROSE

Oh, I suppose you is a doctor, Homer?

HOMER

Almost.

MR. ROSE

I don't need no "almost" a doctor, Homer.

Homer can't bear to watch Rose Rose at work with the needle.

ROSE ROSE

We should drown that damn Jack in the vat!

MR. ROSE

Now, now, darlin' . . . Jack just needs to know what business he's in.

ROSE ROSE

Yeah, you really showed him, Daddy—you just about cut your own hand off, and all you cut off *him* was his clothes!

MR. ROSE

You oughta know you don't go to jail for cuttin' a guy's *clothes*. Ain't that right, Homer?

Homer winces at the stitching.

INT. WALLY'S CAR—DRIVE-IN THEATER—EARLY EVENING

Wally's car comes bouncing along the ditches of the closed drive-in. Homer is at the wheel; Candy calls out some driving instructions. The car comes to a stop next to a speaker-post. Candy leans out; she grabs the speaker and hangs it on the window. Homer sits back and drapes his arms out the window and over the seat. He feels great.

CANDY

You're a natural. You were born to drive a car like this.

HOMER

You think? Maybe I was.
(looks around)
I love this place!

Homer looks up at the giant movie screen.

HOMER *(cont.)*

The screen is enormous! Imagine King Kong up *there*! Have you seen a lot of movies here?

CANDY

Yes . . . and no. When you come here, you don't really care about the movie.

Homer stares at Candy in disbelief.

HOMER

You don't care about the movie?

Candy looks at him for a moment.

CANDY

What are you so crazy about the movies for?

HOMER

It was my favorite night at the orphanage—movie night. We'd race into the dining hall. Of course everyone wanted to sit in front, so we'd be packed in so tight you could feel the kid next to you breathing.

CANDY

At least you were never lonely.

HOMER

I didn't say that. Growing up in an orphanage, you're always lonely. You're just never alone.

Candy is moved. Homer feels exposed; he tries to change the mood by making light of what he's said.

HOMER *(cont.)*

You're not alone in the bathroom, or . . . or in the shower . . . you're never alone in wanting the last piece of meatloaf, or even in your own bed on a cold morning.

Candy laughs.

CANDY

You don't miss it?

HOMER

I miss things. I miss . . . people.
(*with certainty*)
I miss reading to the boys.

CANDY

But you had so much *responsibility*.

HOMER

I never *asked* for any responsibility.

CANDY

Just a little privacy.

Homer laughs.

CANDY *(cont.)*

Privacy is exactly the point of drive-in movies.

HOMER

Did you come here with Wally—to *not* watch movies?

At the mention of Wally they both look a little self-conscious.

CANDY

Sometimes . . . movies mostly bore Wally.

HOMER

Ah-ha.

(points to the speaker)

So what is that—a radio?

CANDY

The *speaker*. For the movie sound.

Candy looks at Homer.

CANDY *(cont.)*

Scrunch down like this.

Candy scrunches down in her seat; Homer imitates her. Homer is focused on the giant screen.

HOMER

How could you not *care* about the movie?

CANDY

You just cuddle. You come to hug . . . to kiss. You don't *come* here to watch the movie.

HOMER

(teasing her)

That's what *I'd* come here for. I'd watch the movie.

CANDY

Not with the right girl you wouldn't.

Homer's expression changes from exhilarated to guilty. He leans back in his seat and looks straight ahead at the screen. Candy tentatively leans her head on his shoulder. Homer looks afraid to breathe.

From behind, with her head on his shoulder, they look like a normal couple. We track in toward the huge screen until we see only the screen. There are shadows on the blank screen. Suddenly the movie King Kong *appears.*

INT. DINING HALL—NIGHT

King Kong *is playing against the bare, white wall. Fuzzy is very weak, but he smiles at the sight of the love-struck Kong holding the screaming Fay Wray in his giant hand. Dr. Larch runs the projector; he sits close beside Fuzzy. When the film breaks in the predictable place, Fuzzy makes no protest. Dr. Larch looks at Fuzzy, who has stopped breathing; his eyes are closed.*

LARCH

Fuzzy? Fuzz?

They are alone in the dining hall. Larch has wheeled in Fuzzy for a private viewing.

EXT. ST. CLOUD'S—GRAVEYARD—MORNING

Buster helps Larch lower the small coffin into the grave. The tiny gravestone says "F. S."

BUSTER

What are you going to tell the little ones?

LARCH

I'll tell them Fuzzy was adopted.

BUSTER

Why would the little ones believe that *anyone* would adopt him?

LARCH

They'll believe it because they want to believe it.

BUSTER

Shouldn't we tell Homer?

LARCH

If Homer wanted to know what was happening here, he could pick up a telephone and call us.

INT. BOYS' DIVISION—NIGHT

The boys in their beds listen to Buster inventing Fuzzy's "family."

BUSTER

It was a family with a better breathing machine than the one Dr. Larch built.

INT. ST. CLOUD'S—CORRIDOR—NIGHT

Larch leans against the wall, covering his eyes, overhearing the boys.

BUSTER (*O.S.*)

The family that adopted Fuzzy, they *invented* the breathing machine. It's their business . . . breathing machines.

Larch pauses; he waits to see if they believe this.

CURLY (*O.S.*)

Lucky Fuzzy!

Larch almost breaks with a sudden sharp breath.

ALL THE BOYS (*O.S.*)

Good night, Fuzzy! Good night, Fuzzy! Good night, Fuzzy Stone!

EXT. CIDER HOUSE—MORNING

As the men sit at the picnic table eating their cornbread, Rose Rose pours coffee. A Jeep comes down the orchard road toward them. It's Olive. Mr. Rose leads the "Good mornin', Mrs. Worthin'ton!" greetings. Olive has an armful of clothing and a fairly sizable package; she brings the latter over to Homer.

OLIVE

Some mail for you, Homer.

Homer shakes the package; he puts the package beside the table, unopened. Olive turns to Rose Rose.

OLIVE *(cont.)*

And some clothes for you, dear—
(nodding to the cider house)
let's go see if they fit.

Mr. Rose watches Rose Rose and Olive disappear into the cider house. The other men view Homer's package with curiosity, especially Peaches.

PEACHES

Ain't you gonna see what it is, Homer?

MR. ROSE

Mind your own business, Peaches.

PEACHES

Sorry, Homer . . .

INT. BUNKHOUSE—LATE AT NIGHT

Homer lies awake in bed; everyone else is asleep. Homer pulls the package out from under his bed, opening it just enough to see what it is; then he shoves it back under his bed.

EXT. OCEAN/BEACH—DUSK

The beach at sunset. Candy and Homer, dressed for cooler weather, are alone at the water's edge. From a paper bag, Candy is scattering some small, brightly colored pieces of broken glass.

HOMER

Aren't you worried that people will cut their feet?

CANDY

Nobody will swim here until next summer. By then, the water will have rubbed the glass smooth against the sand— there won't be any sharp edges.

She finds an old piece of glass among the stones and shells at the high-tide mark.

CANDY *(cont.)*

See? That's last year's glass, or from some year before. I put glass here every year. The ocean makes it beautiful.

Candy holds up a piece of glass to the sun for Homer to look at. The ocean is a gray-green color, the glass a paler shade of green.

CANDY *(cont.)*

Give me your hand.

She rubs the smooth piece of glass against his hand, then throws it toward the water. It falls short. Homer retrieves it. Candy splashes him playfully. He chases her away from the beach, into the pine trees. Homer locks his arms around her, from behind. He can't let go. She lets him hold her, then breaks his grip. She turns to face him. She is taller than he is, older, obviously more experienced. She initiates the kiss. They drop to the ground right there; they make love by the roots of the tree, Candy guiding him.

EXT. WALLY'S CAR—BEACH PARKING LOT—NIGHT

They come out of the woods, walking toward the car, Candy leading. We hear Candy talking just before we see her and Homer.

CANDY

(increasingly upset)
Nobody volunteers for the Burma run—he said so himself. And nobody knows *me* better than him! So how am I supposed to feel? He's a bomber pilot and I'm just selfish, I know. Well, I'm *not* a brave little girl and I'm *not* sorry.

She sits in the passenger seat, Homer in the driver's seat.

CANDY *(cont.)*

I *know* this was right.
(pause)
I told you. I'm not good at being alone.
(pause; in a whisper)
I told him, too.

Homer concentrates on starting the car.

CANDY *(cont.)*

(repeating herself)
I *know* this was right.

HOMER

Right.

Their expressions, as the car pulls away, belie their words.

EXT. CIDER HOUSE—END OF DAY

Homer and Mr. Rose sit opposite each other at the picnic table. Rose Rose stands behind her father, her hands on his shoulders, watching Homer snip out Mr. Rose's stitches—very quickly.

MR. ROSE

Slow down, Homer—don't be in such a big hurry.

HOMER

This is easy—I'm not hurrying.

MR. ROSE

You still doin' it too fast!

Job done, Homer leaves the table and hurries to the bicycle, pedaling away. Rose Rose watches Homer go, as Mr. Rose flexes his healed hand.

ROSE ROSE

He's in a big hurry, all right. I told you he's in trouble.

EXT. CAPE KENNETH—LOBSTER POUND—EVENING

Candy and Homer sit on the dock. Candy still seems to be wrestling with her conscience. Homer throws snails in the sea. It's cold.

HOMER

Just tell me. Do you want me to go? Do you want me to stay?

CANDY

It will be okay.

HOMER

What will be okay?

CANDY

We have to wait and see. I think that, for *everything* in life, you have to wait and see.

Homer throws a snail with more force.

HOMER

I'll just move on, get another job somewhere.

Ray comes out onto the dock; he sees Homer throwing another snail.

RAY

Every time you throw a snail off the dock, you're makin' someone start his whole life over.

Candy throws a handful of snails into the water.

CANDY

Maybe we're doing the snails a favor, Daddy.

Ray looks at the two of them; he sighs.

RAY

It's gettin' late. I think I'll pack it in.

CANDY

Good night, Daddy.

Ray nods good night; he leaves. Homer looks expectantly at Candy.

CANDY *(cont.)*

We'll just have to wait and see.

INT. WORTHINGTON HOUSE, DINING ROOM—NIGHT

Olive and Homer sit at the dining-room table, the remnants of an apple pie in front of them. Homer is still eating. Pictures of Wally are on the wall.

OLIVE

I used to hate it when Wally went back to college—even when it was just college! And this was when his father was still alive . . . I hated it even then. Naturally I hate this more.

Homer nods in sympathy. His mouth is stuffed with apple pie.

OLIVE *(cont.)*

What I mean is . . . I would like it very much if you thought you could be happy here, Homer.

HOMER

(wiping his mouth)
Mrs. Worthington, I feel I'm very lucky to be here.

OLIVE

There's not a lot of work in the winter, and you'll have to tolerate Vernon—even Wally despises him, and Wally likes everyone.

Olive's thoughts drift; her eyes look up at a photo of Wally.

HOMER

I think Wally will be fine, Mrs. Worthington—he seems indestructible to me.

OLIVE

(distracted)
I don't know.
(intently at Homer)
Just promise me one thing.

Homer is tense. Does Olive suspect about Candy?

HOMER

Uh . . . sure.

OLIVE

Just promise me that, if there's a blizzard, you'll move into Wally's room until it's over.

They both laugh, but Homer has a hard time looking her in the eye.

EXT. CIDER HOUSE—DAY

The pickers are moving out; the harvest is over. Olive and Homer stand near the door to the bunkhouse, talking—we can't hear their conversation. Rose Rose and the other men walk past them, carrying the last of their belongings to the truck. Olive and Homer walk over to the truck.

OLIVE

Good-bye. Have a safe trip home. Thank you, again, for all your hard work.

MR. ROSE

You take care now, Mrs. Worthin'ton.

They shake hands.

OLIVE

Good-bye, Arthur.
(she hugs Rose Rose)
Homer, I'll see you tomorrow?

HOMER

Right.

Olive gets in her Jeep and waves as she drives off.

The truck is packed. Muddy tugs on a rope that secures the load.

MUDDY

(to Mr. Rose)
We all set, I think.

Mr. Rose nods and gets in behind the wheel. Rose Rose and Muddy get in next to him. The others are bundled up for the ride in the open back of the truck.

As they're leaving, Homer waves good-bye—the pickers calling out to him.

MR. ROSE

You all take care of yourself, too, Homer!

PEACHES

We see you next harvest.

MUDDY

Don't freeze to death, Homer.

JACK

Go on and freeze to death if you want to, Homer.

MR. ROSE

Now, now, Jack—that just ain't right.

ROSE ROSE

You just stay out of trouble, Homer!

Homer stands looking after them, after they've gone.

INT. BUNKHOUSE—LATER THAT SAME DAY

Homer is alone, rearranging his stuff—spreading out a bit, making the place his own. (On the other beds, we see the mattresses rolled up on the bare bedsprings.)

CANDY *(O.S.)*

So, you're staying.

Homer turns; he hadn't seen Candy come in.

CANDY *(cont.)*

Olive told me.
(awkward pause)
You might have told me yourself.

HOMER

I'm just waiting and seeing. Like you said.

She smiles. He goes to her; they embrace.

BEGINNING A MONTAGE OF THE NEXT NINE OR TEN MONTHS.

EXT. CIDER HOUSE ROOF—MORNING

Homer, drinking coffee, is writing a letter on a note pad.

HOMER (*V.O.*)

Dear Dr. Larch, thank you for your doctor's bag . . .

EXT. RAY'S LOBSTER BOAT—DAY

Homer is learning how to "haul" a lobster pot with Ray and Candy's guidance.

HOMER (*V.O.*)

. . . although it seems that I will not have the occasion to use it.

EXT. LOBSTER POUND, FLOATING PENS—EVENING

Following Ray's example, Homer is trying to "disarm" the lobsters' big claws by blocking them shut with the little wooden wedges. Ray works quickly, never getting pinched. As Candy watches, Homer gets pinched.

HOMER (*V.O.*)

Barring some emergency, of course. I am not a doctor. With all due respect to your profession, I am enjoying my life here.

INT. BUNKHOUSE—NIGHT

Homer and Candy are naked. They have pulled two beds together and made a double bed. He can't take his eyes off her.

HOMER

I've looked at so many women . . . I mean, I've seen *everything* about them, *everything* . . . but I never felt a thing. I felt nothing. Now . . . with you . . . it *hurts* . . . to look at you.

INT. DISPENSARY—DAY

Edna and Angela and Larch are all reading Homer's letter, their lips moving silently as they read the words.

HOMER (*V.O.*)

I am enjoying being a lobsterman and an orchardman—in fact, I have never enjoyed myself as much.

INT. WORTHINGTON HOUSE, FIREPLACE—NIGHT

Olive and Homer and Candy are playing a board game around the fireplace.

HOMER (*V.O.*)

The truth is, I want to stay here. I believe I am being of *some* use.

INT. LARCH'S OFFICE—NIGHT

Edna and Angela view him anxiously from the doorway as Larch furiously types and types.

LARCH (*V.O.*)

My dear Homer, I thought you were over your adolescence, that period which I would define as the first time in our lives when we imagine we have something terrible to hide from those who love us.

INT. WALLY'S CAR—DAY

Candy is singing to the car radio, as animated and happy as we've ever seen her. Homer, driving, can scarcely keep his eyes on the road; he has to keep looking at her.

LARCH (*V.O.*)

Do you think it's not obvious to us what's happened to you?

INT. BUNKHOUSE—NIGHT

With the radio playing (a popular song), Homer hops across the bare floor, pulling on his boxer shorts; he opens the door to Olive, who's holding out an armload of blankets to him. He sheepishly thanks her. When Homer closes the door, we see a hidden (and stricken) Candy, naked from their interrupted lovemaking.

LARCH (*V.O.*)

You've fallen in love, haven't you? By the way, whatever you're up to can't be too good for your heart. Then again, it's the sort of condition that can be made worse by worrying about it. So don't worry about it!

EXT. ORCHARDS—DAY

Vernon and Homer are working under an apple tree; they are poisoning mice.

HOMER (*V.O.*)

Dear Dr. Larch, what I am learning here may not be as important as what I learned from you, but everything is new to me. Yesterday I learned how to poison mice. You use poison oats and poison corn.

INT. DINING HALL—EVENING

Supper chaos—Buster and Mary Agnes are doing their best to stop a food fight while Larch and Angela and Edna are completely absorbed reading Homer's letter.

HOMER (*V.O.*)

Field mice girdle an apple tree. Pine mice kill the roots. I *know* what you have to do—you have to play God. Well . . . killing mice is as close as I want to come to playing God.

INT. MOVIE THEATER—CAPE KENNETH

Homer and Candy are watching Rebecca.

LARCH (*V.O.*)

Do I interfere? When absolutely helpless women tell me that they simply *can't* have an abortion, that they simply *must* go through with having another—and yet another—*orphan* . . . do I interfere? *Do* I? I do not. I do not even *rec-*

ommend. I just give them what they want: an orphan or an abortion.
(close on Homer)
You are my work of art, Homer. Everything else has been just a job. I don't know if you've got a work of art in you, but I know what your job is. You're a doctor!

INT. BUNKHOUSE—DAY

The radio is playing a slow, sexy dance number. The fat ladies from the apple mart are dancing as they paint the interior walls of the bunk room.

HOMER (*V.O.*)

I am not a doctor.

LARCH (*V.O.*)

You know everything I know, plus what you've taught yourself—you're a better doctor than I am and you know it!

Homer is finishing up painting the kitchen walls. When he gets to the list of rules, tacked on the wall, he removes the list and finishes painting under where the rules were.

LARCH (*V.O.*)

They're going to replace me, Homer! The Board of Trustees is looking for my *replacement*!

Two of the ladies unroll the rolled-up mattresses on the bare bedsprings, as Vernon enters with an armload of blankets and pillows.

HOMER (*V.O.*)

I can't replace you! I'm sorry . . .

Homer holds up the list of rules, rereads it briefly; he walks over to an unpainted beam, a support beam, and tacks the rules on this beam.

EXT. CIDER HOUSE, ROOF—MORNING

Homer reads Larch's letter, sipping coffee.

LARCH (*V.O.*)

Sorry? I'm not 'sorry'! Not for anything I've done. I'm not even sorry that I love you!

INT. DISPENSARY—NIGHT

Larch sits on his ether-bed with a letter from Homer in his hand. He looks completely deflated. Angela is standing in the doorway.

LARCH

I think we may have lost him to the world. He's not coming back.

END OF THE MONTAGE.

INT. BUNKHOUSE—EARLY EVENING

In the newly painted, spruced-up cider house, Homer and Candy are dancing to another slow, sexy song on the radio. He is untucking her blouse, feeling under her blouse—she starts to unbutton his shirt. They kiss while they dance. But the song changes abruptly on the radio, to something fast and silly.

Homer responds to the music, dancing goofily—instantly out of the mood. Candy laughs, but she picks up a pillow and swings it at him, hitting him. He dances away from her. She throws the pillow; he ducks—the pillow lands somewhere near the door. Now Homer grabs a pillow and chases her from bed to bed. She shrieks—they're both laughing. They each grab a pillow and stand toe to toe, whacking each other, laughing all the while, until he pins her arms behind her and, breathing hard—and despite the stupid music that broke the mood—they are passionately kissing again.

The sound of a truck is sudden and loud.

EXT. CIDER HOUSE—DAY

Mr. Rose's truck has arrived. The pickers are hopping out of the truck, grabbing their gear.

INT. BUNKHOUSE—DAY

The door opens. Hero and Peaches barge in, as Homer and Candy are struggling to return the pillows to the beds.

HERO

Who's that?

PEACHES

It's that Homer!

Muddy is right behind them. He picks up a pillow, off the floor, looking for which bed it belongs on.

MUDDY

It's that Candy, too . . .

Then comes Mr. Rose, slyly smiling, taking it all in—there's no hiding what going on. Homer and Candy are caught, their shirts untucked and half-

unbuttoned—they're still out of breath. The pillows lie crazily on the beds, each one of which has been stepped on.

MR. ROSE

Don't this place look like home?

PEACHES

It look nicer than home!

MR. ROSE

What have you two been doin' to make it look so nice?

Rose Rose enters. She looks hardened, toughened—not happy. She plops down her stuff on her bed, looking only at Candy.

ROSE ROSE

How is that Wally doing?

CANDY

Oh, he's fine! I just heard from him. He's bombing all these places . . .

Homer tries to help out.

HOMER

(mumbling)

. . . bridges, oil refineries, fuel depots . . .

He peters out, knowing how sick of hearing this Candy is. He tries to change the subject.

HOMER *(cont.)*

Where's Jack?

There is an uncomfortable silence.

MUDDY

He just wasn't up for the trip.

More silence.

MR. ROSE

That Jack just never knew what his business was.

One look at Muddy and we know something pretty bad happened to Jack.

EXT. ORCHARDS—DAY

The pickers on their ladders, all picking. Homer is now a good picker; he looks over at Rose Rose. She is slumped against her ladder, not picking, completely ignoring an argument beneath them in the aisle between the trees. (Mr. Rose is checking over the apples Peaches has just picked.)

MR. ROSE

You pickin' nothin' but cider apples, Peaches—I hope you understand that.

PEACHES

They ain't drops—I picked 'em off the tree!

MR. ROSE

Then you pickin' 'em too fast—they ain't no better than drops to me. See that bruise, and that one? *Half* of these is bruised! Look at this one! It ain't got no stem! You might as well *step* on 'em, too—they only good for cider.

EXT. ORCHARDS—DUSK

In the aisle between the trees, Homer and Candy are arguing in one of the work vehicles.

CANDY

Do you think I'm having a good time? Do you think I'm just *teasing* you? Do you think I *know* whether I want you or Wally?

HOMER

So we should "wait and see." For how long?

CANDY

I grew up with Wally. I began my adult life with him.

HOMER

Fine. That's all there is to it then.

CANDY

No! That's not all there is to it! I love you, too—I *know* I do.

HOMER

Okay, okay—I know you do, too.

CANDY

(bitterly)

It's a good thing I didn't have that baby, isn't it?

Her sudden hardness leaves him speechless as they go their separate ways. Candy drives on.

EXT. CIDER HOUSE—SUNNY MORNING

Breakfast time at the picnic table. Rose Rose sits by herself, away from the table. She does not look well; she suddenly goes back inside the bunkhouse.

PEACHES

(calling after her)

Ain't you eatin' with us, Rose?

PEACHES *(cont.)*

(to the men)

She used to eat with us. Now we ain't good enough for her, I guess.

HERO

She ain't hungry, maybe.

MUDDY

She ain't hungry every mornin' 'cause she's sick every mornin'.

Homer gets up to take his dishes inside.

INT. KITCHEN AND BUNKHOUSE—MORNING

When Homer comes in, Rose Rose is throwing up in the sink.

HOMER

You okay, Rose?

ROSE ROSE

I guess you must like watchin' me be sick . . .

HOMER

I don't like watching anyone be sick.

Rose Rose lies down on her bed with the curtain open. There is something familiar about the way Homer approaches her bedside; he does so with the authority of a doctor. He sits on the edge of her bed with such complete self-assurance that she doesn't protest.

HOMER *(cont.)*

How many months are you?

She just stares. But she doesn't stop him when he touches her abdomen. It's as if she knows that he knows what he's doing.

HOMER *(cont.)*

You're not yet three months, are you?

ROSE ROSE

Not yet. What do you know about it?

HOMER

I know more than I want to know about it. Who's the father?

ROSE ROSE

Don't trouble yourself about it, Homer—this ain't your business.

HOMER

But you don't look very happy.

ROSE ROSE

Happy! What are you thinkin'? How am I supposed to take care of a baby! I can't have a baby.

HOMER

Rose, please listen. Whatever you want to do, I can help you.

She is taken aback.

HOMER *(cont.)*

What I mean is, if you don't want to . . . keep the baby, I know a place where you can go.

ROSE ROSE

You think Daddy's gonna let me go anywhere? I ain't going *nowhere*.

She rolls over on the bed, facing away from him again.

ROSE ROSE *(cont.)*

Why don't you just go back to your pickin', Homer? I can take care of it myself!

HOMER

Rose, listen—don't *do* anything. You know, I mean to yourself. Please listen . . .

MR. ROSE (*O.S.*)

(*calling*)

Homer! Is this a workin' day or what?

EXT. LOBSTER POUND—EVENING

Homer and Candy are sitting at the dock.

CANDY

We should take her to St. Cloud's. That much is obvious, isn't it? Let her make up her mind when she gets there . . .

HOMER

I told her! She doesn't feel she can do that. Something about her father not letting her go anywhere . . .

CANDY

Well, we have to help her!

Homer doesn't respond.

CANDY *(cont.)*

We have to do *something*. Don't we?

(beat)

Homer?

Homer looks out over the ocean; he remains unresponsive.

EXT. CIDER HOUSE—MIDDAY

Rose Rose is setting the picnic table for lunch when Candy arrives.

CANDY

Hi . . .

ROSE ROSE

Hi . . .

She keeps setting the table.

CANDY

I've got some more clothes for you—I just keep forgetting to bring them with me.

ROSE ROSE

I don't need no more clothes, thank you.

CANDY

(softly)

Rose, I know what's going on.

Homer told me. I got pregnant, too—about a year ago.

(pause)

I've been through this.

Rose Rose looks down.

ROSE ROSE

You ain't been through what I been through, Candy.

CANDY

(doesn't get it)

Yes, I *have*!

Rose Rose dismissively waves her hand.

CANDY *(cont.)*

Who's the father, Rose?

Rose looks at Candy and shakes her head.

CANDY *(cont.)*

You want to have the baby?

Rose Rose shakes her head again, more emphatically.

CANDY *(cont.)*

I know where you can go. Homer and I can take you . . .

ROSE ROSE

I can't go nowhere.

CANDY

Why?

Rose Rose stays silent.

CANDY *(cont.)*

Is it the father? Does he know?

Rose Rose turns away from Candy.

CANDY *(cont.)*

You can trust me. Is it Jack? It's not Jack, is it? It's *Muddy*! Is it Muddy?

ROSE ROSE

(almost wistfully)
No. It ain't Muddy. Muddy's just . . .

Rose Rose stops; she can't even continue setting the table. Her voice turns bitter, despairing.

ROSE ROSE *(cont.)*

It sure ain't Jack.

There, suddenly, is Mr. Rose, walking past them. He is uncharacteristically tentative.

MR. ROSE

(to his daughter)
I'll be up top . . .

Mr. Rose leaves Candy and Rose Rose alone again. Rose Rose nods almost invisibly after her father. Rose Rose looks pointedly at Candy, nodding. Candy slowly gets it. Mr. Rose is the father! Rose Rose lets that sink in; she keeps looking at Candy with an ashamed expression.

EXT. ORCHARD—DAY

The pickers are at work, on their ladders, when Candy runs down the aisle between two rows of trees. She stops at the bottom of Homer's ladder, out of breath. Muddy and Peaches and Hero, in the treetops, are watching and listening.

CANDY

She won't go to St. Cloud's!

HOMER

(shrugging)

Well, we can't force her. It's her decision.

CANDY

You don't understand! It's her father . . .

HOMER

Mr. Rose *knows?*

CANDY

(shouting)
He's the *father*! He's her baby's father!

The pickers can't help but hear this, too. Candy starts to leave, Homer running after her.

HOMER

Wait . . . *wait*! Are you sure?

CANDY

We've got to keep her away from that bastard!

Candy leaves. Homer starts looking for Mr. Rose.

EXT. ORCHARD, NEAR CIDER HOUSE—MOMENTS LATER

Smiling his enigmatic smile, Mr. Rose keeps slowly picking while Homer stands at the foot of his ladder.

MR. ROSE

I didn't see where you was pickin' this mornin', Homer, but you musta worked up a big appetite. You look like you're serious about gettin' to your lunch today!

HOMER

Is it true?

Mr. Rose stops picking, his eyes darting to see who's around.

HOMER *(cont.)*

Are you sleeping with your own daughter?

Mr. Rose, with deliberate slowness, comes down the ladder.

MR. ROSE

(slyly; still composed)

I think you been stayin' up too late at night, Homer.

HOMER

You're actually having sex with your own little girl? Is that possible?

MR. ROSE

Ain't nobody havin' *sex* with my little girl, Homer—that's somethin' a father knows.

HOMER

You're lying. How can you . . . with your own daughter!

Mr. Rose switches from sly to threatening in a split second.

MR. ROSE

Homer, don't you know what business you in? You don't wanna go into no business with me, Homer—ain't that right?

HOMER

Go on, cut my clothes. I've got other clothes.

Mr. Rose is indignant.

MR. ROSE

You a fine one to be talkin' about lies. Shame! These people took you in. That boy Wally's at *war*!

That takes some of the steam out of Homer's superiority.

HOMER

But she's your *daughter* . . .

MR. ROSE

And I *love* her! There ain't nobody else gonna treat her as good as I do!

(looks away)
I wouldn't do nothin' to hurt her, Homer—you must know that.

Homer turns; he speaks over his shoulder as he walks away.

HOMER

She's *pregnant*. Do you know *that*?

By his expression—he looks as if he's been punched—it's clear that Mr. Rose didn't *know that.*

The other pickers are on their way to lunch; it's obvious that Muddy, Peaches, and Hero already know that Mr. Rose is sleeping with his daughter.

EXT. CIDER HOUSE—PICNIC AREA—LUNCHTIME

Rose Rose is sitting at the picnic table when the pickers arrive for lunch, almost simultaneously with Homer. He looks at, then looks away from, Rose Rose. Mr. Rose is the last to sit down at the table as a very tense, wordless lunch begins.

EXT. ORCHARD—DAY

Homer is on a ladder picking apples. Muddy climbs a ladder on the other side of the same tree.

MUDDY

Don't mess in this, Homer, if you know what's good for you.

HOMER

How long's this been going on, Muddy?

MUDDY

Long enough. You ain't gonna stop it.

Muddy looks all around for Mr. Rose; then he gives Homer his knife.

MUDDY *(cont.)*

There's my knife, Homer. It ain't gonna do *me* no good. You give that knife to Rose Rose, you hear?

Homer nods, pocketing the knife. As Muddy climbs down and moves his ladder to an adjacent tree, he keeps talking to Homer until he disappears in the leaves.

MUDDY *(cont.)*

You best just watch your ass, Homer! You don't wanna end up like Jack!

Homer thoughtfully continues his work.

INT. BUNKHOUSE—LATE AT NIGHT

Homer lies awake in his bed.

EXT. ORCHARD—LATE AFTERNOON, ANOTHER DAY

The pickers on their ladders in the trees; nobody is talking. In the late sun, the leaves have a reddish, fiery glow.

EXT. ORCHARD—ANOTHER DAY

It's much colder; the pickers are on their ladders in the trees again, but they're dressed for the cold. Homer is high on a ladder; he turns toward the view of the Worthington house when he hears a car come to a screeching halt in the driveway. Homer sees Candy get out of Wally's car; she leaves the door open and runs toward the house. Parked in front of Wally's car is an Army Jeep, with an ENLISTED MAN *leaning against it. The indifferent soldier smokes a cigarette as he watches Candy run.*

CANDY

No! No!

Homer descends the ladder and runs for the house, down an aisle between the rows of trees. The pickers watch him run.

INT. WORTHINGTON HOUSE, LIVING ROOM—DAY

Camera follows Homer into the Worthington house where, from the front hall, he sees Olive and Candy (in profile) sitting on the couch. We can't see who's talking, nor do we recognize the voice. As Homer comes into the living room, we see MAJOR WINSLOW *sitting in a chair (also in profile), talking to Olive and Candy.*

Major Winslow is a smooth, handsome, well-briefed officer in the casualty branch of the Army Air Corps; he's done his homework, but he's not all business. He's painfully aware of the delicate nature of his report.

MAJOR WINSLOW

When the plane was hit, the crew chief and the radioman jumped close together. The copilot jumped third. All on Captain Worthington's orders—the captain was still flying the plane. None of the men on the ground could see the sky—that's how thick the jungle was. They never saw the plane crash—they never *heard* it crash. They never saw Captain Worthington's parachute, either.

OLIVE

Why was he missing for twenty days?

MAJOR WINSLOW

Because the crew thought he'd gone down with the plane. They were hospitalized for almost a week in China before they were flown back to India. It wasn't until then that they sorted through their gear . . .

CANDY

Who cares about their *gear*?

MAJOR WINSLOW

Three men jumped from the plane, but they had four compasses with them. One of the crew jumped with Captain Worthington's compass.

CANDY

He was in Burma for twenty days without a compass?

MAJOR WINSLOW

He followed the Irrawaddy River, all the way to Rangoon. Somehow he managed to avoid the Japs, but not the mosquitoes.

OLIVE

Then it's malaria?

MAJOR WINSLOW

It's encephalitis B. He's recovering at Mount Lavinia Hospital, Ceylon.
(pause)
Uh . . . Captain Worthington is paralyzed.
(Olive gasps)
Waist down. He won't walk.

Candy stands and leaves the room.

MAJOR WINSLOW *(cont.)*

(to Olive)
I'm sorry.

HOMER

(asks the major)
There are no autonomic effects, are there?

Major Winslow has to consult his notes.

MAJOR WINSLOW

No autonomic effects . . . that's correct.

OLIVE

When will he be home, Major?

MAJOR WINSLOW

Four weeks or so, right around Halloween.

INT./EXT. WALLY'S CAR—LOBSTER POUND—END OF DAY

Homer and Candy are sitting in the parked car in silence.

HOMER

(finally)

There are no autonomic effects, just the paralysis of the lower extremities.

Candy stares at him, uncomprehending.

HOMER *(cont.)*

Wally can have kids, a normal sex life . . .

Candy cries.

EXT. LOBSTER POUND—EVENING

Ray is throwing snails in the water. Candy sits on the end of the dock, slumped on Homer's shoulder.

RAY

How about him not needin' the friggin' compass! How about that?

CANDY

Daddy, *please* . . .

Ray knows that she wants him to leave. He shuffles off the dock, toward the house. He knows how they both must feel.

RAY

Good night, kids. Don't catch cold—it's gettin' cold already.

CANDY

Good night, Daddy.

HOMER

Good night, Ray.

Homer tries to cuddle closer, but Candy sits up, preoccupied.

HOMER *(cont.)*

Just tell me. I'll do whatever you want to do.

CANDY

Nothing.

HOMER

Isn't that like waiting and seeing?

CANDY

No. Nothing is nothing. I want Wally to come home. I'm afraid to see him, too.

HOMER

I know.
(he kisses her)
Is *that* nothing?

CANDY

No, don't—that's something. Nothing is nothing.
(Homer's sad smile)
Don't even look at me. I want . . .

Candy buries her face in his chest.

CANDY *(cont.)*

. . . to do nothing.

Homer holds her, doing nothing, while she sobs. As her crying subsides, Homer's thoughts are far away. With Candy slumped against him, hugging him, he doesn't look at her; instead, he looks out to sea and at the darkening coast, Candy's words resonating. An unfamiliar expression is on his face.

HOMER

(mumbling to himself)
It's a tempting idea, I know . . . to do nothing.

Candy is silent. Homer feels strangely agitated; he shifts his position.

CANDY

(groans)
Please don't move, don't go anywhere.

HOMER

(overly genuine)
Go anywhere? Of course not! That would be *doing* something, wouldn't it? We wouldn't want to *do* something. Let's just sit here all night!

CANDY

(irritated)
If you're trying to be funny, Homer . . .

HOMER

(irritated, too)
I'm not trying to be anything—I'm just doing nothing! If I wait and see long enough, then—with any luck—I won't *ever* have to make up my mind! Decisions can be painful, after all . . .

Candy is angry; she gets to her feet and stares hard at him.

CANDY

Stop it! Just cut it out!

HOMER

(mock surprise)

You got up! You *did* something! If you keep this up, you might be in danger of making a *decision*!

CANDY

For God's sake, Homer, Wally's been shot down!

Candy sobs. Homer puts his face in his hands for a minute. He regains his composure and stands up.

HOMER

(genuinely contrite)
I know, I'm sorry.

CANDY

(yelling and sobbing)
He's *paralyzed*!

HOMER

(deadpan; just the facts)
He's *alive*. He still loves you.
(pause)
So do I.

CANDY

(anguished)
What do you want me to *do*?

He faces away from her.

HOMER

(with calm resolve)
Nothing. You're not the one who has to do anything.

EXT. CIDER HOUSE—NIGHT

Homer is in semidarkness as he walks toward the cider house.

MR. ROSE (*O.S.*)

Where do you think you're going?

ROSE ROSE (*O.S.*)

You gotta to let me go, Daddy. Please . . .

Homer walks faster. When he gets to the cider house, he sees Mr. Rose and Rose Rose arguing. Rose is sitting on the bicycle, a bundle of her clothes tied up behind the seat.

MR. ROSE

You ain't goin' nowhere in the middle of the night, girl!

ROSE ROSE

I ain't your business no more, Daddy. Please let me go.

Rose Rose starts to pedal away, but Mr. Rose stops her. She starts to struggle.

HOMER

Hey, hey! Stop it. Maybe I can help.

They turn to see Homer.

MR. ROSE

You just go on inside, Homer. We don't need no help.

ROSE ROSE

That's right, Homer. This ain't your business.

She tries to break free from her father and pedal away, but he stops her again. They keep struggling.

HOMER

Please listen to me! *Both* of you . . .

MR. ROSE

You forget yourself, Homer. This here's my daughter!
You got your own mess to deal with—ain't that right?

Homer steps between them, which makes Mr. Rose furious.

MR. ROSE *(cont.)*

(yelling)

What business is you in, Homer?!

HOMER

Mr. Rose, I'm in the *doctor* business.

(to Rose Rose)

If you want, I can help you. You don't have to go anywhere.

Rose Rose and Mr. Rose stop struggling. Suddenly Homer is in charge.

INT. BUNKHOUSE—NIGHT

Muddy, Hero, and Peaches smoke in their beds. Rose Rose opens her curtain and peers out from her bed. She gets up and goes toward the kitchen area in her nightshirt; she stops at an unused bed, now covered with white rubber sheeting—Homer's medical intruments are displayed and ready. Homer finishes scrubbing his hands in the sink. His surgical mask is loosely tied around his neck.

Mr. Rose is looking at Homer's surgical instruments when Rose Rose joins him.

MR. ROSE

(to Homer)

What's that? What's it called?

HOMER

One cervical stabilizer, two sets of dilators—Douglas points. One medium-sized curette, one small; one medium speculum, one large; two vulsellum forceps.

MR. ROSE

There ain't no *almost* about this stuff, Homer—ain't that right?

Homer ignores him; he keeps naming his equipment.

HOMER

Merthiolate, ether, vulval pads, gauze—lots of gauze.

MR. ROSE

When it comes to this, you is the real thing—is that what you sayin'?

Homer looks at Mr. Rose and Rose Rose.

HOMER

No *almost* about it—I'm a doctor.

Homer turns to Peaches, Hero, and Muddy.

HOMER *(cont.)*

Get out of here, please.

Muddy herds Peaches and Hero out of the bunkhouse.

MR. ROSE

I'm stayin', Homer.

HOMER

Okay. Then you can be of use.

INT. BUNKHOUSE—NIGHT

Mr. Rose wears a surgical mask; he is sweating, even in the cold, and his eyes look stricken as he watches Homer, who is performing the abortion. Mr. Rose holds the ether cone over Rose Rose's face. He drips some ether from the bottle on the cone.

Cut quickly from Rose Rose's etherized face . . . to Mr. Rose's eyes above his mask . . . to Homer working with his eyes trained on the speculum . . .

EXT. CIDER HOUSE—NIGHT

. . . to Muddy and Peaches and Hero huddled under the overhanging roof in the rain.

INT. BUNKHOUSE—NIGHT

Mr. Rose is having a hard time breathing.

HOMER

You better get some air.

EXT. CIDER HOUSE—NIGHT

The cider house in the rain. Mr. Rose staggers out; he stands there in the rain, trying to regain his composure. He starts to scream.

Another angle: huddled under the overhanging roof, Muddy and Peaches and Hero are watching him.

INT. BUNKHOUSE—RAINY DAY

Rose Rose, curled in a fetal position, listens to the rain on the roof. Candy sits on her bed beside her. She helps her to sit up, to drink a glass of water; then Rose Rose lies down again. Rose Rose's expression never changes while Candy talks to her. Mr. Rose lies in his bed in the exact same fetal position as his daughter; he, too, is listening to Candy. Homer is putting away his instruments.

CANDY

The bleeding should taper off tomorrow, but it can come back again. The cramps will ease up, almost entirely. The bleeding is usually much lighter in two days. As long as the bleeding isn't heavy, it's normal.

Muddy enters the cider house from out of the storm. He glances at Candy and Rose Rose; then at Homer. Then he speaks to Mr. Rose.

MUDDY

It's that Vernon—he keeps askin' where you and Homer and Rose Rose is at.

MR. ROSE

Tell that Vernon to mind his own business, Muddy.

MUDDY

I told him that you all is sick.

MR. ROSE

Tell him what you want, Muddy—*you* is the crew boss today.

Hero and Peaches, dripping wet, come inside. Peaches is standing next to the list of rules tacked to the kitchen support beam.

PEACHES

Look at that. Them same damn rules is tacked up again!

Homer has finished putting his instruments away.

MUDDY

Why don't you put them damn rules in the wood stove, Peaches?

As the men are murmuring their approval of this idea, Rose Rose interjects.

ROSE ROSE

I want to hear what they are, first.

The men groan, but Mr. Rose won't oppose his daughter on this subject—not this time. He just lies there.

ROSE ROSE *(cont.)*

Homer, let me hear what they are.

Homer begins to read.

HOMER

"One: Please don't smoke in bed."

MUDDY

We heard that one already, Homer.

HOMER

"Two: Please don't go up to the roof to eat your lunch."

PEACHES

That's the best place to eat lunch!

HOMER

"Three: Please—even if you are very hot—do not go up to the roof to sleep."

HERO

What do they think? They must think we're crazy!

MUDDY

They think we're dumb niggers so we need dumb rules—that's what they think.

HOMER

This is the last one.

The men groan, in mock disappointment.

HOMER *(cont.)*

"Four: There should be no going up on the roof at night."

PEACHES

Why don't they just say, "Stay off the roof!"?

HERO

Yeah, they don't want us up there *at all*!

Homer crumples the list and throws it into the wood stove.

ROSE ROSE

(to Homer)
That's *it*?

HOMER

That's it.

ROSE ROSE

It means nothin' at all! And all this time I been *wonderin'* about it!

PEACHES

They're *outrageous*, them rules!

MR. ROSE

Who *live* here in this cider house, Peaches? Who grind them apples, who press that cider, who clean up the mess, and who just plain *live* here . . . just breathin' in the vinegar?
(he pauses)
Somebody who *don't* live here made them rules. Them rules ain't for *us*. *We* the ones who make up them rules. We makin' our *own* rules, every day. Ain't that right, Homer?

HOMER

Right.

Camera closes on Candy.

INT. / EXT. WALLY'S CAR—DRIVE-IN THEATER—EVENING

Homer and Candy sit and stare at the blank screen; they don't look at each other. Candy grips the steering wheel of the parked car.

CANDY

Please don't make me say it again.

HOMER

No, that's not it—I just want to be sure I understand you.

Candy slumps forward with her forehead on the steering wheel.

HOMER *(cont.)*

I *helped* you not to think about Wally. You were so upset—you couldn't stand worrying about him, about his being killed and not coming back—but when you were with me, you could stop worrying . . . well, for a while, anyway. This is how I helped you, right?

CANDY

Please . . . that's enough. I *loved* you, too—you know I did.

HOMER

". . . did." Well, okay.

CANDY

Please don't . . .

HOMER

(sarcastically)
And now that Wally's coming back, and because he'll certainly *need* you . . .

CANDY

You say that as though it's some awful thing!
(angrily)
I never stopped loving Wally!

Homer lets that sink in.

HOMER

(still sarcastic)
At least there's no more waiting and seeing. At least I got to see the ocean.

Candy covers her face in her hands and cries uncontrollably, unstoppably. Homer's anger keeps him impervious to her tears—another "first" for him. He turns and looks at her with an almost clinical curiosity; then he goes back to staring at the blank screen.

EXT. ORCHARD—IN FRONT OF THE APPLE MART—DAWN

The rain has stopped but the grass is wet, the trees glistening in the dawn light as Wally's car stops and Homer gets out. The car exits the frame in one direction; Homer, walking, exits the frame in another.

EXT. CIDER HOUSE—DAWN

As he walks toward the cider house, Homer sees Muddy and Peaches and Hero waving to him from the roof.

MUDDY

Rose Rose has runned away!

PEACHES

She took off in the night!

MUDDY

She took off on the bicycle, man.

Homer starts jogging, then running toward the cider house. Muddy comes down the ladder to meet him.

INT. BUNKHOUSE—EARLY MORNING

Rose Rose's bed is exposed. The curtains are flung open; her bed is empty. Mr. Rose is still in his bed, in the fetal position we have seen before. Mr. Rose's trancelike expression doesn't change as Homer and Muddy enter.

MR. ROSE

Ain't nobody gonna find her, Homer—she's long gone.

(pause)

I swear, I didn't try and stop her—I just wanna touch her hand before she go. That's all I wanna do, I swear.

(pause)

Where'd she get that knife, Muddy? That looked like *your* knife—what I seen of it.

Muddy is scared; he looks to Homer for advice.

MR. ROSE *(cont.)*

If that was your knife, Muddy, I wanna thank you for givin' it to her—no girl should be goin' *hitch-hikin'* if she don't got a good knife with her.

HOMER

(seeing the blood)

Where'd she get you?

MR. ROSE

She just plain misunderstand me—I was tryin' to give her my knife, I was just reachin' to touch her hand. But I understand if she misunderstand me—it's all my fault, ain't that right?

Homer takes the blanket off him; Muddy gasps. Homer tries to examine Mr. Rose's wound. Mr. Rose smiles at him.

MR. ROSE *(cont.)*

It's too late for the doctor now, Homer—ain't that right?

Homer doesn't answer; he knows Mr. Rose is a goner.

MR. ROSE *(cont.)*

(proudly)

She's *good* with that knife! She's real fast. She's a lot better with that knife than *you* is, Muddy! And who do you suppose taught her?

MUDDY

You taught her, I suppose . . .

MR. ROSE

That's right! A girl's gotta know how to defend herself, don't she?

He winces in pain at Homer's examination.

HOMER

(surprised)

There's more than one laceration, more than one cut.

MR. ROSE

That's 'cause I sticked my *own* knife in the wound—after she go, I sticked my *own* knife in there. I poked it all around, I just tryin' to find the same place she got me.

Homer finds Mr. Rose's knife. There's blood everywhere.

MR. ROSE *(cont.)*

You listen to me: you tell them police how this happen, you tell it *this* way, you hear? My daughter, she runned off—and I so sad about it that I stabbed myself. I so unhappy that she gone, I killed myself—that what you say, you hear? That the true story—ain't that right?

Homer and Muddy exchange a glance. Mr. Rose, with his blood-soaked hand, suddenly grabs Homer by the throat.

MR. ROSE *(cont.)*

Let me hear you say that! I so unhappy she runned away that I killed myself—that what happen here, ain't that right?

HOMER

Right.

MUDDY

That what happen—you lost your only daughter so's you killed yourself! That's what we say, all right.

MR. ROSE

That's right. I know you understand how I feel, Homer—you is breakin' them rules, too. Ain't that right?

Mr. Rose dies. Muddy turns away. Homer closes Mr. Rose's eyes.

EXT. CIDER HOUSE, ROOF—MORNING

Muddy and Hero and Peaches are sitting close together on the roof, like banished children. It is from their perspective that we see the police car and the ambulance—two men carrying the body out of the cider house, and a cop or two talking to Homer and Olive, and Homer talking to them. We hear no dialogue.

EXT. APPLE MART—DUSK

Homer and the men load crates of apple jelly onto a truck. The mood is solemn; they work with tired focus. Candy drives up. The men are evasive with her; they find a reason to work across the mart. Candy walks to Homer, stands next to him. They say nothing for a moment, until Candy breaks the silence.

CANDY

Do you think she'll be all right?

HOMER

She knows how to take care of herself.

Candy looks away; she can't think of what to say. She shoves her hands into her pockets, finds a letter there, which she hands to Homer.

CANDY

This came for you a couple of days ago. Olive asked me to bring it. With everything happening, I guess she forgot.

HOMER

Sure. Thanks.

Homer looks at the letter from St. Cloud's; he puts it unopened in his pocket, without a second thought. Candy can't let things end there.

CANDY

I know you don't think much of being needed, or of me for that matter . . .

HOMER

I'm sorry for what I said about Wally needing you. It was . . . unnecessary.

CANDY

No, I'm the one who should be sorry. You have every right to be angry.

HOMER

No. You warned me. I didn't listen, but you warned me.

Candy looks surprised.

HOMER *(cont.)*

You told me you weren't any good at being alone.
(pause)
You told Wally, too. Right?

Candy can only stare straight ahead.

HOMER *(cont.)*

(relenting)
He's going to be fine, Wally's going to be fine. I know he is.

A tear rolls down Candy's cheek, Homer wipes it away; then he stops touching her and looks off into the quiet orchards.

INT. BUNKHOUSE—NIGHT

The pickers lie in their beds, smoking. Homer is undressing. He pulls the letter out of his pocket and sits down on his bed. Homer opens the letter without enthusiasm and begins to read.

ANGELA (*V.O.*)
Dear Homer, I am writing to tell you about Wilbur.

INT. DISPENSARY—NIGHT

Music is playing on the old phonograph as an exhausted Larch gives himself ether.

INT. GIRLS' DIVISION—NIGHT

Edna is getting the girls ready for bed. Music continues Over.

INT. DISPENSARY—NIGHT

Larch has twisted himself on the narrow bed so that his face is unusually close to the windowsill, and when the ether cone starts to fall off his face—and his slack hand trails down, off the side of the bed—the cone becomes caught against the windowsill.

He tries to turn his face away from the cone, but he presses his face into the sill—thus holding the ether-soaked cone over his mouth and nose. His hands twitch, he's trying to wake up; the hand that holds the ether bottle lets the bottle fall. The bottle shatters against the sill; the ether spreads, running red with blood from a cut on Dr. Larch's hand or finger. Music continues Over. It's a funeral.

INT. CORRIDOR—NIGHT

Buster is bringing in the wood as the music plays Over. Buster smells the spilled ether. He heads toward the dispensary, sniffing. Camera follows him into the dispensary.

In the dispensary: Buster approaches Larch's ether-bed.

BUSTER

Dr. Larch? Dr. Larch?

He drops the armload of wood and runs for help.

INT. DISPENSARY—NIGHT

Angela enters. She feels for Larch's pulse; Larch is dead. Angela opens a window. She pulls Larch's body away from the windowsill. Buster joins her on the bed.

ANGELA (*V.O.*)

I can assure you that the overdose was entirely accidental.

INT. BUNKHOUSE—NIGHT

Homer finishes reading the letter; he puts it down, gets up, and walks to a window. He stares into the night.

ANGELA (*O.S.*)

Let us be happy for Dr. Larch. Dr. Larch has found a family.

THE BOYS (*O.S.*)

Good night, Dr. Larch! Good night, Dr. Larch! Good night, Dr. Larch!

Homer wipes a tear off his cheek.

EXT. PICKERS' TRUCK—CIDER/PACKING HOUSE—MORNING

The truck is packed for the long trip south; it passes by the packing house, which looks closed for the season. No one else is about. Muddy is driving slowly, his arm out the open window. In the back, huddled among their belong-

ings, are Peaches and Hero (on one side) and Homer (on the other). The pickers are trying to draw Homer into their conversation, while Homer is giving the apple farm a good-bye look. He has made up his mind about something.

MUDDY

You ever see a palm tree, Homer?

PEACHES

He ain't never been outta Maine!

HERO

Ain't you sick of pine trees, Homer?

Homer just smiles and shakes his head.

EXT. WORTHINGTON HOUSE, DRIVEWAY—MORNING

As the pickers' truck drives past, Homer is on the side of the truck nearest the Worthington house and driveway; he sees Olive and Candy and Ray helping Wally out of the car and into a wheelchair. A NURSE *stands by.*

Wally is wearing what appears to be an oversized officer's coat or flight jacket, his face looking small in the overlarge clothes. He can't move his legs at all, and his mouth is drawn into a tight-lipped smile.

PEACHES (*O.S.*)

Let me tell you somethin' about Florida, Homer.

HERO (*O.S.*)

The Sunshine State!

PEACHES (*O.S.*)

It's so nice 'n' warm down there, you can pick them grapefruits and oranges *naked*, if you want to.

Olive is dissolved in tears. Candy is sobbing; she kisses Wally, without ceasing, while he haltingly touches her face, her hair.

In the truck, the smile is gone from Homer's face. He shakes his head.

HOMER

Thanks, guys . . . I'd like to go with you. But I've got to move on.

MUDDY

Yeah, well . . . you could move on with *us*, man! You could move on somewhere *warm*!

PEACHES

Homer, stayin' in Maine ain't movin' on!

This makes all the pickers laugh, but Homer just smiles and shakes his head. He watches the Worthington house disappear from view.

INT. MOVING TRAIN—PASSENGER CAR—NIGHT

A CONDUCTOR, *taking tickets, comes to Homer, who is better dressed than we've ever seen him; he is looking at his sober reflection in the black window-glass of the night train when the conductor gets his attention. When the conductor moves on, Homer takes Angela's letter out of his breast pocket; he skips ahead to the end.*

ANGELA (*V.O.*)

Dr. Larch often wondered how the world was treating you.

EXT. ST. CLOUD'S—GRAVEYARD—AFTERNOON

ANGELA (*V.O.*)

He talked a lot about you, hoping you would be of use, whatever you were up to.

Angela and Buster and Mary Agnes and Edna carry Larch's coffin; they set it down by the raw hole. The pile of fresh dirt stands out against the new snow; the hole is black against the new white.

EDNA (*O.S.*)

"Oh Lord, support us all the day long . . ."

We see the wheelbarrow with the gravestone.

EDNA (*O.S.*)

". . . until the shadows lengthen and the evening comes, and the busy world is hushed, and the fever of life is over, and our work is done."

INT. GIRLS' DIVISION—NIGHT

We see the faces of the girls praying for Larch (Mary Agnes, too) as Edna finishes her favorite prayer.

EDNA

"Then in Thy mercy grant us a safe lodging, and a holy rest, and peace at the last."

INT. MOVING TRAIN—PASSENGER CAR—NIGHT

Camera closes on Homer, sleeping to the sound of the rocking train. Angela's letter lies in his lap.

THE GIRLS (*O.S.*)

Amen! Amen! Amen!

EXT. ST. CLOUD'S—TRAIN STATION—EARLY MORNING

The train stops, blowing snow. Homer steps off the train carrying a suitcase and Dr. Larch's bag. The disapproving stationmaster is still disapproving. Music plays Over, something triumphant.

EXT. ST. CLOUD'S—THE HILL—EARLY MORNING

Homer makes his way up the hill toward the orphanage. Music Over.

EXT. ORPHANAGE—EARLY MORNING

Edna is breaking up fights; this time, instead of fighting over snowballs, the orphans are fighting over their pumpkins. Suddenly Homer tops the brow of the hill and they all see him. Buster is the first to catch sight of Homer; he runs toward him. Mary Agnes also sees Homer; she immediately turns away and runs inside. Music FADES OUT *Over.*

INT. LAVATORY—EARLY MORNING

Mary Agnes crashes into the bathroom and stumbles up to the mirror; she starts to fix herself up with shaking hands.

INT. ORPHANAGE, FRONT HALL—EARLY MORNING

Everyone has heard the news; they come on the run. The children flock around Homer, hugging him. Homer takes Angela and Edna in his arms. Mary Agnes joins the group. Homer takes in how changed, how attractive she is. They smile awkwardly at each other.

INT. BOYS' DIVISION—EVENING

Homer's suitcase is open on the bed; we see Homer's hands as he begins to unpack. Smaller hands reach in and root through the clothes.

CURLY *(O.S.)*

Did you bring something for me?

Curly continues his search. Homer thinks for a second; then he reaches into his pocket and pulls out the piece of pale-green glass.

HOMER

You know what? I did.

Homer hands the piece of glass to Curly.

HOMER *(cont.)*

It's from the ocean. It's for you.

Curly is duly impressed; he walks away to examine his new teasure. Homer continues unpacking. He pulls his X ray out and puts it aside.

BUSTER

What are you doing here?

Homer turns to see Buster, Mary Agnes, Angela, and Edna in the doorway.

MARY AGNES

We made up a room for you.

ANGELA

Wouldn't you be more comfortable by yourself?

Homer smiles; he nods.

Angela and Mary Agnes start to put Homer's things back in his bag. Edna picks up the X ray and looks at it with a somber expression.

EDNA

Homer, do you know what this is?

HOMER

Sure. It's my heart.

ANGELA

(shakes her head)
Actually, it's Fuzzy's. There's nothing wrong with your heart.

HOMER

Fuzzy's?!

EDNA

Dr. Larch wanted to keep you out of the war, Homer—that's why he did it. That's why he told you it was yours.

Homer is stunned; he puts his hand to his heart.

ANGELA

I think he worried about his own heart. He said it would never stand up to Homer Wells going off to war.

Homer takes that in; he nods. Mary Agnes touches him sympathetically.

INT. LARCH'S OFFICE—NIGHT

Homer looks at his fake diplomas; they are now framed and hanging on the office wall. Homer surveys the office, as if for the first time; he sits down in the desk chair, as if slowly getting used to his new position.

INT. BOYS' DIVISION—NIGHT

Homer reads to the boys from David Copperfield. *While his voice is strong—positive, optimistic, certainly reassuring to the boys—there is in the conclusion of the chapter something that distracts him. He seems to hesitate; he misses a line or two, and perhaps he purposely skips one or two others. (Possibly Homer's eyes wander ahead, to the title of the next chapter: "I Make Another Beginning.")*

HOMER

"Thus I began my new life, in a new name, and with everything new about me. . . . I felt . . . like one in a dream. . . . The remembrance of that life is fraught with so much . . . want of hope. . . . Whether it lasted for a year, or more, or less, I do not know. I only know that it was, and ceased to be; and . . . there I leave it."

Homer stops and looks at the boys' faces.

CURLY

What happens next?

Homer smiles.

HOMER

That's tomorrow, Curly. Let's not give the story away.

Homer puts out the lights and leaves the boys in the familiar semidarkness. Seconds later, the closed door to the hall is flung open, flooding the room with light from the hall, and Homer, dressed in his long white laboratory coat and looking every inch the doctor, *delivers his best imitation of Larch's popular blessing.*

HOMER *(cont.)*

Good night, you Princes of Maine! You Kings of New England!

On Copperfield and Steerforth and Curly as the door to the hall is closed and semidarkness prevails in the room again. Copperfield, smiling, shuts his eyes. After a second, the wide-eyed Steerforth shuts his eyes, too. Then Curly.
The last to close his eyes is Buster.

FADE TO BLACK.

MIRAMAX FILMS *Presents*
A FILMCOLONY *Production*
A Film By LASSE HALLSTRÖM
TOBEY MAGUIRE
CHARLIZE THERON
DELROY LINDO
PAUL RUDD
and MICHAEL CAINE

THE CIDER HOUSE RULES

JANE ALEXANDER
KATHY BAKER
KIERAN CULKIN
KATE NELLIGAN
HEAVY D
K. TODD FREEMAN
PAZ DE LA HUERTA
and introducing ERYKAH BADU
Casting by
BILLY HOPKINS
SUZANNE SMITH
KERRY BARDEN
Music by
RACHEL PORTMAN
Costume Designer
RENÉE EHRLICH KALFUS
Editor
LISA ZENO CHURGIN
Production Designer
DAVID GROPMAN
Director of Photography
OLIVER STAPLETON, B.S.C.
Co-Producers
ALAN C. BLOMQUIST
LESLIE HOLLERAN
Executive Producers
BOB WEINSTEIN
HARVEY WEINSTEIN
BOBBY COHEN
MERYL POSTER
Screenplay by
JOHN IRVING
Based upon his novel
Produced by
RICHARD N. GLADSTEIN
Directed by
LASSE HALLSTRÖM

CAST

Homer Wells	TOBEY MAGUIRE
Candy Kendall	CHARLIZE THERON
Mr. Rose	DELROY LINDO
Wally Worthington	PAUL RUDD
Dr. Wilbur Larch	MICHAEL CAINE
Nurse Edna	JANE ALEXANDER
Nurse Angela	KATHY BAKER
Rose Rose	ERYKAH BADU

Buster	KIERAN CULKIN
Olive Worthington	KATE NELLIGAN
Peaches	HEAVY D
Muddy	K. TODD FREEMAN
Mary Agnes	PAZ DE LA HUERTA
Ray Kendall	J. K. SIMMONS
Jack	EVAN DEXTER PARKE
Vernon	JIMMY FLYNN
Hero	LONNIE R. FARMER
Fuzzy	ERIK PER SULLIVAN
Curly	SPENCER DIAMOND
Copperfield	SEAN ANDREW
Steerforth	JOHN ALBANO
Hazel	SKY MCCOLE-BARTUSIAK
Clara	CLARE DALY
Major Winslow	COLIN IRVING
Carla	ANNIE CORLEY
Adopting Father	PATRICK DONNELLY
Adopting Mother	EDIE SCHECHTER
12 yr. old girl	KASEY BERRY
Big Dot	MARY BOGUE
Debra	VICTORIA STANKIEWICZ
Florence	CHRISTINE STEVENS
Dr. Holtz	EARLE C. BATCHELDER
Mrs. Goodhall	NORMA FINE
Stationmaster	JOHN IRVING
Stunt Coordinator	CHARLIE CROUGHWELL
Utility Stunts	BILL MORTS
	DENNEY PIERCE

CREW

Unit Production Manager	BARBARA A. HALL
First Assistant Director	STEPHEN P. DUNN
Second Assistant Director	TINA STAUFFER

Associate Producers	LILA YACOUB
	MICHELE PLATT
Art Director	KAREN SCHULZ-GROPMAN
Camera Operator	CHRIS LOMBARDI
First Camera Assistant	DOUG SCHWARTZ
Second Camera Assistant	RANDY STONE
Add'l. Camera Assistants	SCOTT RESSLER
	KEVIN SCHMIDT
Loader	SHAYNA RITENOUR
Assistant Art Directors	PETER ROGNESS
	KIM JENNINGS
Set Decorator	BETH RUBINO
Art Dept. Coordinator	WYLIE GRIFFIN
Leadman	SCOTT BOBBITT
Buyer	KATHY ROSEN
Leadman-Maine/Set Dresser	ARTHUR WOOD
Set Dresser/Fixtures	TYRIS SMITH
Set Dressers	CHRIS FOUSEK
	RICHARD OESER
	PHYLLIS PENFOLD
Draper	HOLLY LAWS
Art Dept. Production Asst.	RANDY MANION
Location Manager	CHARLES HARRINGTON
Asst. Location Manager	MARK FITZGERALD
Location Assistants	KERRY FITZMAURICE
	LUKE RAMSEY
	SVEN DAVISSON
Script Supervisor	JANE GOLDSMITH
Location Casting	MARTY CHERRIX
Location Casting Assistant	MANNY POULOS
N.Y. Casting Associates	JENNIFER MCNAMARA
	MARK BENNETT
L.A. Casting Associate	DEBORAH MAXWELL-DION
N.Y. Casting Assistant	SIG DE MIGUEL
Production Supervisor	DIANA ZOCK
Production Coordinator	MARIANNE CRESCENZI

Production Accountant	APRIL JANOW
Asst. Production Accountant	JILL HAHN
Second Asst. Accountant	CHERYL MILLER
Payroll Accountant	LAURA KREFT
Accounting Clerk	BRANDON HOLLYER
Property Master	SANDY HAMILTON
Assistant Property Master	DANIEL BOXER
Assistant Props	KRIS MORAN
Associate Costume Designer	LIZ SHELTON
Wardrobe Supervisor	BARBARA HAUSE
Key Set Costumer	KEITH LEWIS
Set Costumer	MARGARET PALMER
Seamstresses	JONI HUTH
	CASSY MCEVOY
Additional Costumers	SUSAN ANDERSON
	GRETCHEN SCHLOTTMAN
	LISA LESNIAK
Wardrobe Production Asst.	CAMILLE RUSTIGE
Key Hairstylist	PEG SCHIERHOLZ
Assistant Hairstylist	BRENDA MCNALLY
Ms. Theron's Hairstylist	WAYNE HERNDON
Ms. Badu's Hair Consultant	DIHANN GREEN
Key Makeup Artist	ELLIE WINSLOW
Assistant Makeup Artist	SHARYN CORDICE
Ms. Theron's Makeup Artist	DEBORAH LARSEN
Production Sound Mixer	PETUR HLIDDAL
Boom Operator	CARL FISCHER
Sound Utility	RYAN WEBB
Gaffer	ANDY DAY
Best Boy Electric	MIKE REED

LAMP OPERATORS

SARAH BLACK   JENNY KANE

ROBERT CUDDY WAYNE SIMPSON
ROGER MARBURY

Rigging Gaffer LON CARACAPPA
Rigging Best Boy BRIAN PITTS
Rigging Electrics PATRICK RUTH
JAMES MITCHELL

Key Grip BOB ANDRES
Key Rigging Grip MATT MILLER
Best Boy Grip MIKE DILESO
Rigging Best Boy MARK WEIL
Dolly Grip RICH KEREKES

GRIPS
ALISON BARTON DARREL L. TEMPLE
ERIC KOMAR SARCO KIRKLIAN

Greensman STEPHANIE WALDRON
Greens Foreman JEFF DEBELL
Greens Assistants RICH BELL
DAVID GODFREE

Special Effects Coordinator RON BOLANOWSKI
Special Effects ROBERT BOLANOWSKI

Assistant to Mr. Gladstein SOPHIE MCMENAMIN
Assistant to Mr. Hallström EDIE SCHECHTER
Assistant to Mr. Irving CHLOE BLAND
Assistant to Mr. Cohen WILL SWEENEY
2nd Second Asst. Director PAUL PRENDERVILLE
DGA Trainee MELISSA RUDMAN
Key Set Production Asst. DENNIS DOYLE

SET PRODUCTION ASSTS.
MICHAEL JACOBSON ALASDAIR MACLELLAN
CHAD LEMIEUX PHILLIPPA WEAVER
Production Secretary CODY ZWEIG
Office Production Assts. NATHAN FORD
COLBY ENDERS

	SARAH ELLIOT
Film Runner	TIMOTHY BROOKS
Assistant to Mr. Maguire	LISA MANTOUX
Assistant to Ms. Theron	ARLENE PACHASA
Assistant to Mr. Lindo	HANK THOMAS
Mr. Caine's Dialect Coach	JESS A. PLATT
Unit Publicist	RACHEL ABERLY
Unit Stills Photographer	STEPHEN VAUGHAN
Construction Coordinator	RODNEY ARMANINO
Construction Foreman	ALAN ALLINGER
Local Construction Foreman	TED SUCHECKI
Labor Foreman	FRANCIS FOLEY
Maine Foreman	ERIC MATHESON
Metal Fabricator	EUGENE POPE
Construction Office Manager	JONATHAN MARTIN

CARPENTERS

JONATHAN ASKEW	JUDSON BELL
WILLIAM BERGLAND	STEVE DEBOER
JAMES FAULKNER	TIM JACKSON
EDWIN JAMES SCOTT JR.	CAMERON MATHESON
ROBERT MCKOWN	STEVE MORRELL
ALEXANDER NESBIT	CHRISTOPHER NOONAN
DAVID NORTH	DAVID ROTUNDO
WILLIAM SALTER	PETER ST. ONGE
PETER WILCOX	PAUL WILLIAMSON

BRIAN WOODS

Construction Prod. Asst.	LORETTA WADE
Master Scenic	BOB TOPOL
Camera Scenic/Lead	M. TONY TROTTA

SCENIC ARTISTS

RAND ANGELICOLA	DOUG CLUFF
DAN COURCHAINE	JOHN HAVEN STORY
SUE PETERSON	KEVIN SCIOTTO
Transportation Coordinator	JIMMY FLYNN
Transportation Captain	RICHARD ABATE

DRIVERS

RICHARD ABATE JR.	DENISE AVALLON
DAVE BOSTIC	RICHARD BUTTERO
ROBERT CARNES	TOM COSTLEY
WILLIAM COYMAN	JOHN CRONK
RICK DESTASIO	NICK DILORETTO
ROBERT DUDLEY	DAVID DUGGAN
WILBUR ELLIS	JERRY GUARINO
ROGER HITCHCOCK	BOBBY MARTINI
JACK MCBRIDE	RODERICK MCCELLAN
MARIO PRESTERONE	FRANK ROSSI
BART SMALL	RICHARD VILLIARD

STAND-INS

NYDIA COLO'N	PAUL HARRINGTON
RICK JOHNSTON	GEORGE JONES
SHERRY KOFTAN	LARRY PRICE
JIM SLABACHESKI	PAM SOUTHWICK

MIKE SURGEN

Set Medic	DEB CLAPP
Catering by	DELUXE CATERING
Chef	LORIN FLEMMING
Catering Assistants	JAMES FLEMMING
	JUAN RUIZ
	GERRY HERNANDEZ
Craft Service	SUE CHRISTY
Asst. Craft Service	JENNIFER ROBERTS

Studio Teachers	KELLY KEOUGH
	DEBRA REES
Projectionists	JIM PLAZA
	ED O'NEIL

POST PRODUCTION

Post Production Supervision	POST PRODUCTION PLAY-GROUND

KATIA MILANI

First Assistant Editor MAY KUCKRO

Second Assistant Editor SANDRA NASH

Apprentice Editors TEREL GIBSON

PAUL WAGTOUICZ

Assistant Post Supervisor MICHAEL WILLIAMS

Supervising Sound Editor MAURICE SCHELL, M.P.S.E.

Music Editor DAVID CARBONARA

Asst. Music Editor JOHN CARBONARA

Sound Effects Editors RICHIE P. CIRINCIONE

EYTAN MIRSKY

Foley Editors BRUCE KITZMEYER

JACOB RIBICOFF

LOU BERTINI

Supervising Dialogue Editor LAURA CIVIELLO

Dialogue Editors BITTY O'SULLIVAN-SMITH

DAN KORINTUS

MAGDALINE VOLAITIS

Supervising ADR Editor GINA R. ALFANO

ADR Editors HARRY PECK BOLLES

MARISSA LITTLEFIELD

Supervising Assistant Sound Editor JAY KESSEL

Assistant Sound Editor JOSHUA LANDIS

Assistant ADR Editor LYNN SABLE

Apprentice Sound Editor BYRON WONG

Re-Recording Mixers STEVE PEDERSON

TOM PERRY

BOB CHEFALAS

Re-Recording Facility TODD-AO STUDIOS EAST

Recordist BOB OLARI

Editorial Facility SOUND ONE CORP.

Post Accounting PREP SHOOT POST

Post Accountants ELIZABETH SPECKMAN

DON MINK

ADR/Foley Recording	SOUND ONE CORP.
ADR Mixer	DAVID BOULTON
ADR Recordist	ALEX RASPA
Background Vocals	DAVID KRAMER'S LOOPING GROUP
Foley Artist	BRIAN VANCHO
Foley Mixer	JOE DOHNER
Re-Recording/Foley	PETER WAGGONER
	FRANK NORRONE
Re-Recording/Previews	DOM TAVELLA
Dolby Sound Consultant	ERIC A. CHRISTOFFERSEN
Special Visual Effects	EYE CANDY
Visual Effects Supervisor	AL MAGLIOCHETTI
Main & End Titles Designed By	NINA SAXON/NEW WAVE ENTERTAINMENT
Titles & Opticals	HOWARD ANDERSON CO.
Negative Cutters	CATHERINE RANKIN
	CHAD GLASTONBURY
Color Timer	CATHY RAIT
Dailies By	DUART

MUSIC

Score Produced By	RACHEL PORTMAN
Orchestrator	RACHEL PORTMAN
	JEFF ATMAJIAN
Engineer	CHRIS DIBBLE
Contractor	GEORGE HAMER
Copyist	TONY STANTON
	BILL SILCOCK
Auricle	CHRIS COZENS
Conductor	DAVID SNELL
Pianist	JOHN LENEHAN
Assistant to Rachel Portman	ELENA GAVRILOVA
Music Recording Studio	CTS STUDIOS, LONDON

Music Consultant BETH ROSENBLATT
Miramax Music Executive RANDY SPENDLOVE

"Ukulele Lady"
Music by Richard Whiting,
Words by Gus Kahn
Performed by
Vaughn DeLeath
Published by Bourne Co.
(ASCAP)/Whiting Music Corp.
(ASCAP)/Gilbert Keyes Music
(ASCAP) c/o SGA
Courtesy of
Columbia Records
By Arrangement with
Sony Music Licensing

"My Ideal"
Composed by Newell Chase/
Leo Robin/Richard Whiting
Performed by
Margaret Whiting with
Billy Butterfield &
His Orchestra
Published by
Famous Music Corp. (ASCAP)
Courtesy of Capital Records
Under License from
EMI-Capitol Music
Special Markets

"Song of the 30's"
Composed by Jerry Mengo
Performed by
Jerry Mengo & His Orchestra
Published by
Cypress Creek Music (ASCAP)
Courtesy of Promusic, Inc.

"King Kong
Original 1933 Score"
("The Snake" —"The Bird"—
"The Swimmers")
Composed by Max Steiner
Performed by
The Moscow Symphony,
William Stromberg, Conductor
Published by Bourne Co.
(ASCAP)
Courtesy of
NAXOS of America

"Alligator Crawl"
Composed by
Thomas "Fats"' Waller
Performed by John Lenehan
Published by
Edwin H. Morris & Company,
A Division of MPL
Communications, Inc. (ASCAP)/
Bienstock Publishing Co.
(ASCAP)
obo Redwood Music Ltd.

"All I Want Is
Just One Girl"
Composed by
Leo Robin/Richard Whiting
Performed by Gus Arnheim's
Coconut Grove Orchestra
Published by
Famous Music Corp. (ASCAP)
Courtesy of the RCA Records
Label of BMG Entertainment

"Count My Fingers" Composed by Jack Trombey	Published by Rouge Music Ltd. (ASCAP) Courtesy of DeWolfe Music Ltd.

Soundtrack on Sony Classical

Production Legal Services	O'MELVENY & MYERS, LLP
Production Attorneys	ERIC ROTH
	SCOTT PACKMAN
Camera Equipment	CAMERA SERVICE CENTER
Prod. Electric Equipment	HOLLYWOOD RENTALS
Add'l. Lighting Equipment	PRODUCTION ARTS
Production Equipment	HADDAD'S, INC.
Travel	DISNEY TRAVEL,
	JANICE JACOBS
Payroll Services	ENTERTAINMENT PARTNERS
Insurance Services	GREAT NORTHERN
	REIFF INSURANCE

"King Kong" Footage Courtesy of
Turner Entertainment Co.

"Rebecca" Footage Courtesy of Buena Vista Film Sales,
A division of Buena Vista International, Inc.

Newsreel Stock Footage Courtesy of
WPA Film Library and Historic Films

"Wuthering Heights" Artwork Courtesy of
MGM CLIP + STILL

VERY SPECIAL THANKS TO

LAURI GLADSTEIN
LENA OLIN
JANET TURNBULL IRVING

BOB OSHER
CARY MEADOW
ANDREW MONDSHEIN
JOSH SILVER
TRACEY JACOBS
BOB BOOKMAN
J.J. HARRIS
ERIC KRANZLER
LESLIE SIEBERT
STEVE DONTANVILLE
TONI HOWARD
RANDI MICHEL
CLARK HENDERSON
STUART FORD
ERIC SHONZ
PRISCILLA COHEN
TOM MCGUIRE

&

IN MEMORIAM
NILS HALLSTRÖM
ULF BJÔRCK
PHILLIP BORSOS

THE FILMMAKERS ALSO WISH TO THANK

Massachusetts Film Office,
Robin Dawson & John Alzapiedi

Vermont Film Office,
Loranne Turgeon

The National Park Service,
Norm Dodge

Jeff Dobbs

Venfort Hall Association,
Tjasa Sprague &
Marcia Brown

Scott Farm—Brattleboro,
Vermont

Commonwealth of
Massachusetts D.C.A.M.,
Robert Cohen

Northampton State Hospital,
Dr. Mark Mitchell,
Bob Melky &
Al "Scottie" Scott

Dr. Laurence Lundy—OB/GYN

Dr. Verneda Lights-Sagay

Dr. Denise Galinas

Massachusetts Governor,
Paul Cellucci

Maine Film Office,
Lea Giraldi

The Town of Northampton,
Massachusetts;
Mayor, Mary Ford

Green Mountain Railroad,
Jerry Hebda

Thurston's Lobster Pound
Bernard, Maine;
Michael Caldwell

The Willis Wood Family

Massachusetts Department
of Corrections,
Bob Balfour

Enterprise Rent-A-Car

Pleasant Street Video

Ed Reilly

Dr. Richard Halgin

David Lennick,
Efrem Productions

Filmed on Location in
Northampton & Lennox, Massachusetts;
Acadia National Park, Maine
and Brattleboro, Vermont